THE VAMPIRE AND THE WANDERING JEW

by

BARAK A. BASSMAN

Cover designed by Telemachus Press, LLC

Cover art:
Copyright © canstockphoto49934207_JohnNorth

Published by Telemachus Press, LLC
7652 Sawmill Road
Suite 304
Dublin, Ohio 43016
http://www.telemachuspress.com

ISBN: 978-1-951744-26-7 (eBook)
ISBN: 978-1-951744-27-4 (Paperback)

Library of Congress Control Number: 2020910602

FICTION/Fairy Tales, Folk Tales, Legends & Mythology

Version 2020.06.08

Table of Contents

THE VAMPIRE AND
THE WANDERING JEW

I. The Monk's Arrival

BROTHER NICHOLAS WAS surprised when he reached the castle gates: everything here was splendid and rich from the perfectly cut square stone blocks of the high outer walls, with not a hint of wear or decay, to the vaulting towers inside made entirely from blindingly bright marble, to the carefully wrought silver statues of lions and boars that adorned the gates.

Such wealth was a stark contrast to the surrounding countryside. Traveling unpaved roads littered with larvae-infested animal carcasses and hard brown weeds, he had seen hardly any livestock, and the fields had only a few meager crops struggling to stay alive in the dusty winds. The peasants had seemed barely alive—stooped, emaciated specters limping about with big saucer eyes who mumbled angry monosyllabic responses to any question.

But then he had come upon this castle, his final destination, with riches beyond compare. At least here would be a decent meal and a warm bed.

After he had stated his business and introduced himself, the gates were opened and a handsome, well-dressed man in the prime of his youth bounded out to greet him. He led Brother Nicholas to Lady Catherine's private chapel, where he would lead Mass and other prayers for the household. This chapel was likewise marvelous to behold—vaulted stone archways, exquisite white marble statues of the Virgin and Child, and carefully etched, brightly colored stained glass panels depicting the story of the Book of Judith (although Brother Nicholas was taken slightly aback by the much too voluptuous images of Judith's figure as she tempted and then beheaded the wicked pagan general, Holofernes).

The handsome youth then brought him to his spacious apartments right above the chapel, which had been thoughtfully fitted out with an ample wooden desk and a lavishly illustrated Latin Vulgate Bible. Tired from his travels, he collapsed into the soft sheets of his new bed and slept until it was time for the evening meal.

Dinner was served in the great hall in a vermillion marble tower. Brother Nicholas was amazed at how young and beautiful everyone was—every courtier and lady in waiting seemed to be no older than twenty-five (at the most) yet possessed of an easy, instinctive grace. He felt painfully aware of the pockmarks and creeping wrinkles on his face. But he was soon distracted by the evening's greatest marvel: Lady Catherine herself, mistress of the castle and ruler of these lands.

Brother Nicholas had learned from the Bishop in the capital of the Duchy of W that she had been widowed more than forty years earlier, shortly after her marriage to the lord of this castle. There were rumors of murder, but nothing was ever proven. After her husband's death, Catherine had refused all offers to remarry, shunned her family and neighbors, and lived in seclusion. The post of her confessor had been vacant for many years before Brother Nicholas had accepted this assignment, in an attempt to flee from his own troubled past. He had braced himself to serve a decrepit, embittered old woman, sad, lonely, and beaten down by years wasted in grim solitude in this bleak country. Perhaps a woman concerned now for her eternal soul as death loomed nearer and in need of spiritual guidance.

Yet Lady Catherine did not look old in the slightest—not a single wrinkle or strand of grey hair—but instead she was tall and erect, with a head of thick, luxurious black hair pinned up in the back and shimmering smooth skin; she glowed with beauty. But while not old, she did not seem young either. There was something heavy about her manner; she had none of the lightness or fresh excitement of youth.

She commenced eating and drinking without any acknowledgement of her new confessor sitting to her left. There was silence for several minutes, until a dashing young man walked up to Catherine, kneeled, and said softly, My Lady, may I present Brother Nicholas, of the Holy Order of _____, who has traveled here, pursuant to his appointment by His Holiness the Bishop, to be the castle's new confessor.

Lady Catherine turned her head to Brother Nicholas and gave him a gracious welcome, asked polite and superficial questions about the journey, and nodded vacantly in response to his bland comments about the bumpiness of the road and the chance to meditate privately in his carriage upon the beauty and goodness of the Lord's creation.

She commented how fine it would be to have regular Mass at the castle's chapel again. It had been many years, she noted, since a priest had set foot within these walls.

Brother Nicholas now felt emboldened to ask whether Her Ladyship would be seeking confession soon, as the long absence of a priest must have delayed her in seeking absolution for her sins.

She smiled and laughed. My dear Brother Nicholas, how very eager you are—how very, very forward. Alas, I have too much to confess. It will take me some time to arrange my sins in proper order. You will have to be patient and start with the porters and the washerwomen.

Then she clapped her hands and demanded a musical accompaniment to her meal. Four handsome young men stood up, held hands, and launched into a song. Brother Nicholas at first thought it sounded lovely. But when he noticed Lady Catherine and her youthful court smirk and stifle their giggles, he concentrated harder on the words. It was a peasant song of some kind, about a girl, young, a floozy—she was drunk. She was apparently going to fornicate in a … he could not make out clearly in a what.

The laughter grew louder, and he noticed guilty, gleeful eyes stealing quick glances at him. Feeling embarrassed, although he could not say why, Brother Nicholas focused harder on the lyrics. It soon became clear to him what was so funny: the drunken floozy was fornicating with a monk in his cell in an abbey.

Furious, he bolted up from his seat, and said, loud enough to rise above the singing, that he was quite tired from his journey and wished to go early to bed. Another elegant, handsome youth—he could not tell them apart, they were all so blonde and fresh and pretty—escorted him out and back to his rooms.

Unable to sleep, he lit a candle and sought the comfort of the divine word of the Old Testament, which he had dearly loved ever since he was a small boy listening to his father recount its tales and wise sayings. He turned to 3 Regum in the Vulgate Bible, to the tale of how the Prophet Elijah in ancient Israel had vanquished and humiliated the wicked, licentious Queen Jezebel and her priests of the pagan demon Baal. Elijah's triumph soothed his angry, raging nerves.

Brother Nicholas then said his nighttime prayers and was about to give himself over to sleep, when he heard a loud, agonizing scream. Startled, he walked over to a window facing the interior courtyard between the castle towers and the gates. The night was dark, with no moon and no torches lit, even on the battlements where Brother Nicholas would have thought there would be armed sentries patrolling.

As no one else seemed to have noticed the loud scream, he wondered if he had imagined it. He truly did need a good night's rest to clear his mind—these were the Evil One's tricks to confound sleep and scramble a man's reason.

So he lay down in bed, closed his eyes, and waited for sleep to swallow him up.

But then he was awoken by another scream, just as loud, but lasting much longer this time. Growing concerned, and not fully trusting the people of this castle, he lit a candle and went outside into the courtyard.

Although he could not see more than a few inches ahead, he slowly followed the direction of the anguished cries. Brother Nicholas gingerly made his way to another tower. The suffering man had to be in this building—his shrieks were deafening by its walls—and yet no one else seemed to notice, much less try to help him.

Feeling his way around the exterior walls he came to a barred window, through which he could see, by a faint light inside, the silhouette of a naked man with a long beard chained to a wall as if he were mounted upon a cross—he was the one screaming. There were two women with him, but they were fully clothed. One held a short spear which she drove into the man's ribcage, similar to how, Brother Nicholas thought, the Lance of Longinus had pierced the ribs of our Lord Jesus Christ on the cross. The other woman held a large bowl or dish of some kind in which she was catching the blood gushing from the man's chest.

Before he could call out to them to stop, Brother Nicholas felt a hard metal stick hit his leg, and he crashed to the ground. Then a blunt object beat down upon his head and he lost consciousness.

II. Black Mass

THROUGHOUT THE NEXT week, Brother Nicholas tried to settle into a comfortable routine. He conducted Mass regularly in the chapel, and he heard confession. But his congregation was meager—a tiny handful of elderly servants, the only old people whom he had seen in what was otherwise a sea of youthful, lovely, mocking faces. His new parishioners clung to him with a feverish desperation, begging him to expound at length upon the Divine Word and to tell them tales from the Bible and the lives of the saints and martyrs. They came up with excuses to linger in the chapel, pretending to have misplaced or forgotten this or that small item.

They were even more agitated in the privacy of confession. These good people had few actual sins to confess—mostly petty jealousies or stealing an extra bite of bread—but they were terrified that they were damned to everlasting torment and their souls stained with the most horrific crimes.

But why are you afraid? Brother Nicholas would ask. You have confessed your sins, which were not so terrible that God in His abounding mercy will not forgive you. Be at peace, and focus your thoughts on His goodness and His love for all His creatures, including you.

Yet his words failed to comfort them. His congregants would tremble and sob and beat themselves with their bony, wrinkled fists, insisting all the time that they were cursed and bound for Hell.

So he would ask them again: Why are you so despairing? It is a great sin to doubt God's ability to forgive and love.

And they would eventually answer: Because we have chosen to stay here in this castle. They insisted there was something unholy, unnatural, about the Lady of the Castle and her unfailingly beautiful courtiers, although they could not say just what crimes had been committed.

Years ago, they would continue, when their lord was still alive and well, the castle was a modest, worn down stone structure, but the surrounding fields were bursting with life—crops, livestock, birds, flowers, and fruits. And then His Lordship, may his soul rest eternally in Heaven, married her. And then he was dead within the year.

Her Ladyship never remarried, but sank all her wealth into building soaring marble towers. Workmen would arrive from who knows where, strange people who would not look you in the eye, and they made the castle into a luxurious pleasure palace. But at the same time the countryside fell into desolation in exact proportion as the castle grounds bloomed into splendor.

The priest who had been her late husband's confessor often fought with Lady Catherine—the old servants had no idea what about, but the Holy Father was very angry, they said, red in the face and shaking—until she drove him away. There had been no priest for so many years that they had worried they would die without absolution for their sins. But now Brother Nicholas, bless his soul, had finally come in answer to their prayers.

Why don't you leave? he would ask them.

Because we fear the poverty of the countryside. Everyone out there, beyond the walls, is starving. In here, we fill our bellies with fine food and sleep on soft sheets. We are greedy gluttons who have put our bodies before our immortal souls, please forgive us, but we fear hunger and disease.

We know there is something wicked here: The Lady Catherine has not aged a day in decades—how can that be natural? And these beautiful maidens and youths, they too never age. Please tell us that God will forgive us for staying in a place like this, with people like this.

Brother Nicholas shared their apprehensions. Lady Catherine and her retinue did not rise from bed until the late afternoon. Despite his entreaties, she refused both communion and confession. She would approach him closely, lean forward so that her long, fragrant black hair grazed his cheeks, and say in a mock-solemn voice that she had far too much on her conscience to know where to begin confessing her sins.

The nights brought him no peace. He tried to convince himself that the vision of the tortured man on the cross was a dream, or a hallucination conjured by a demon, but the next two nights he heard the same awful, piercing cries. He huddled close against his blanket and prayed for guidance.

On the fourth night, it was quiet. However, no longer accustomed to sleeping easily, Brother Nicholas tossed and turned until he decided to soothe his nerves with a walk. He dressed, exited the tower to the inner courtyard, and then mounted the steps to the ramparts of the outer walls. To his surprise, there were no sentries posted anywhere. Such a lavishly rich fortress, he thought, any group of brigands could storm and loot to their heart's content—so why hadn't such a tempting target fallen long ago?

The night was warm but not humid, with a bright moon reflecting against the marble towers. He heard something in the distance. Following the direction of the sound to the edge of the walls, he saw on the ground below a group of lovely young men and women, led by Lady Catherine, walking silently towards the woods with torches in their hands and solemn expressions on their faces. The two maidens whom he had seen torturing the bearded, gaunt man were carrying the broad serving bowl together now, the same one in which they had caught the blood spurting from his ribcage.

The group soon disappeared into the forest and he could no longer see them. He tried to wait for their return, but, overcome by sleep, he returned to his bed.

The same scene repeated the next night, and the night after.

He finally decided to follow them, secretly, to see what was happening in these nighttime gatherings; perhaps this could explain the strange behavior of the inhabitants of the castle.

Instead of going to bed that evening, he went to the ramparts and waited. Once he saw Lady Catherine again leading her procession through the gates, he slipped down the stone steps and followed them from a discreet distance.

They followed a path that led into the woods. The place was dismal: even though it was summer, the trees had barely any leaves, and even less fruit, and there were no birds or animals about.

They stopped at a clearing. Everyone sat down on the ground except Lady Catherine, who stood in the center of the semi-circle of seated attendants. The serving bowl was placed in front of her, and she was handed a richly bejeweled goblet.

Lady Catherine addressed the group: We are gathered here tonight to celebrate Mass to our true lord, who loves and guides us, the one from whom we receive youth and beauty, the one from whom we receive wealth and abundant food. I present to you the body, which represents death and decay— which represents how our forefathers were betrayed and expelled from the Garden of Eden, and forced to eke out a meager living from the unforgiving ground while their wretched flesh withered and wasted away with disease and old age. Join me and curse the body.

Reaching into her cloak, she cast a fistful of communion hosts upon the ground. Then she crouched over them, loudly urinated, and stepped aside. Each member of her congregation likewise rose in turn and similarly desecrated the sacred host. When they were all finished and seated once more, Lady Catherine spoke again:

And now I present to you the blood, which gifts us with youth and beauty, wealth and abundance. And we have been blessed with no ordinary blood, but the blood of the Wandering Jew, who was cursed to eternal wandering by the false god of death and decay. Yet from that curse comes the power to restore life to its original glory, the splendor of life as it was lived in the Garden of Eden. Drink and complete your holy sacrament.

She dipped the goblet into the bowl and drank. Her congregants then each in turn rose again and drank their full. When the perverse communion had been completed, Lady Catherine directed her handmaidens to pick up the bowl again. In the reflected moonlight, Brother Nicholas could see that the bowl was still quite full, even though so many had drunk from it; he shuddered at the thought that they had taken so much blood from the poor Wandering Jew.

In grave silence, the group now walked in a procession out of the woods and back towards the castle. But he did not want to follow them anymore. He sat down on the sparse, dry grass by the trunk of a broad old tree and thought about what he had seen. Such dark, wicked souls in such beautiful, radiant bodies—proof beyond doubt, if he had needed it, of the vanity and deception of the physical world. Her Ladyship had clearly been ensnared by some demon or other.

He had not asked the Bishop why this post had been vacant for so long, so eager had he been to get away from his own troubles. Nor had the Bishop volunteered any information; no, the Bishop had only offered his heartfelt gratitude that a good, self-sacrificing monk had been willing to travel to such a remote wasteland. He remembered the Bishop's words: Brother Nicholas, this is a noble deed, to sacrifice every luxury and comfort to tend to those living in such an impoverished, distant place. You are a credit to the Jews, proof that there is still some good left in them after they betrayed and murdered our Lord upon the cross.

That last remark had smarted.

Exhaustion now overcame Brother Nicholas. He had witnessed enough marvels for one night, he decided, and now he needed to rest and pray for guidance. Once his mind was clearer in the daylight he would decide what to do. So he stood up and followed the path back to the castle.

As he walked, he remembered the first time he had learned about demons. He had been a small boy, perhaps three or four years old. His mother had just given birth to his little sister Miriam. He had loved her instantly—she was so tiny and soft, and she squeezed his finger when he placed it into her palm. He seized upon any chance to help his mother and grandmother with the baby, cleaning her diapers, washing her, and so on and so forth.

He told his friends in their courtyard all about his new baby sister. A mean, wicked boy who was a few years older—what was his name? Shlomo?—had said: You better be careful, because Lilith likes to eat little babies. Maybe Lilith will eat Miriam.

He had run home crying to his mother. She took him in her arms, hugged him tightly, and stroked his hair. Yossele, my beautiful Yossele, why are you crying? Why are you so frightened, my sweet little bird?

Mame, will Lilith eat Miriam? Shlomo said Lilith will eat Miriam. Who is Lilith? Why does she want to hurt Miriam?

Sh, sh, his mother cooed, Miriam is safe. Lilith is a terrible, evil demon, the queen of the demons, but we are safe from her. Come, I will show you.

She held his hand and led him to the threshold of the front door. She then picked him up in her arms so that his head was near the top of the doorway.

See, Yossele, there is our *mezuzah*.

He looked at the miniature rectangular wooden box nailed to the top of the doorpost, with the Hebrew letter *shin* painted in blue on its front. He reached out his hand, touched the *mezuzah*, and kissed his fingers, just like his *tate* did each time he entered the house. His mother smiled and laughed.

Very good, Yossele, just like a big boy would do, she said. And do you know why the *mezuzah* is so important that we must honor it so when we enter our house? Because the sacred Hebrew words in the scroll inside, the words of the Holy One, Blessed be He, are so powerful that they stop any demons, including Lilith, from entering the house. That is why Miriam is safe.

For a fleeting moment, he wished his bedroom in the castle had a *mezuzah* on the doorpost. But this childish whim filled him with shame. He had long given up those ways. What would the Bishop have said to that?

III. The Devil's Acolytes

THE NEXT MORNING Brother Nicholas awoke later than usual, although he washed and dressed quickly enough that he was still able to sing the morning Mass on time. But his soul remained deeply troubled. His congregants were right: there was something wretched and wicked about this place. Yet he was not sure what to do.

Should he remain to try to save and comfort whatever souls struggled against Lady Catherine's evil ways? But then he would be encouraging them to reconcile themselves to life amidst such sin, and doing nothing to curb Her Ladyship's conduct. He might even find himself unwittingly protecting her by making it appear to outsiders that all was well, as, after all, he was there to provide spiritual guidance on behalf of the Holy Church.

Should he flee with the few good Christians among the old servants? That would be cowardly. And where would they go? Those old servants would be left to starve in the barren countryside with whatever family they had left, which had likely long forgotten them and would surely resent suddenly having another mouth to feed.

Of course, for me, his thoughts continued, I will return to the very troubles that drove me to seek this refuge.

He should boldly confront Lady Catherine, he concluded, denounce her abominable heresy and many crimes, and demand she confess, repent, and beg the Lord's mercy and forgiveness. That was his duty.

But he did not want to confront her. While he was repulsed by her behavior, he still felt uncomfortable at the thought of causing her pain or sorrow. There was something about her graceful, confident manner that attracted him, and he was scared that a harsh rebuke, even if justified, would drive her away from him.

Brother Nicholas decided to dine that night at her table, rather than eat alone in his rooms, in the hope that he could learn something new to help guide him. When Lady Catherine entered her hall for dinner that evening, looking rested and refreshed, she asked one of the handsome young men whether any letters had arrived bearing news from elsewhere in the Duchy. He answered that there was a dispute between two of her relatives about who owned the rights to hunt in a certain forest and who was the wrongful poacher—they together having apparently slaughtered almost all the deer in the area— and there were now several petitions and lawsuits and the like. Lady Catherine grew visibly bored and began to pay exaggerated attention to her fingernails. The young man stopped speaking in mid-sentence and sat down.

She called for her meat and wine, and mocked her foolish relations—always squabbling, always haggling over each tiny sliver of land, passionately grasping at any obscure legal precedent to make ever so slight, barely perceptible increases in their estates.

And for what end? she continued. So they can rot inside finer, richer tombs? And even before they die, their ageing bodies will shrivel up like prunes, their skin overrun with blotches and sores, uglier and more disgusting by the moment. But their bony, quaking fingers will still try to grab that one last property deed.

The maidens and the young men heartily concurred in this condemnation of Lady Catherine's greedy, decrepit old relatives.

Brother Nicholas, what do you say? Do you think my relations are fools? Or sinners? What is God's take on the matter?

This was the first time that evening that she had acknowledged his presence. He had been feeling invisible, which he had found surprisingly pleasant: feeling no pressure to correct or scold or instruct, he could simply delight in watching this haughty, beautiful creature, like an immense fluttering butterfly. But now he felt he had been wrong to enjoy Lady Catherine's appearance too greatly, and he re-minded himself again of what she had done, so unholy, the previous night. Straightening himself in his chair and clearing his throat, he tried to answer Her Ladyship with fitting words of guidance and instruction:

My Lady, we are all sinners. It is only through divine grace that we can be saved, a divine gift of mercy that we do not merit. Worldly passions are always in vain. The flesh will rot and decay, and the deceptive luxuries of this brief life will slip away like a half-remembered dream when the Angel of Death comes for you—and then what will be left is the only thing that is truly real, your immortal soul. As the wise King Solomon taught: *Vanitas vanitatum, vanitas vantitatum, et omnia vanitas! Quid habet amplius homo de universe labore suo quo laborat sub sole?* In the common tongue: Vanity of vanities, all is vanity, what benefit can a man truly gain from his labor under the sun?

This is why we must tend to our souls, now, while we still have the chance to be saved. We must nurture and cleanse our souls, and prepare them for the time when they will escape the prison of the body and ascend to the true realm of the Lord to be judged on their merits. I worry, my Lady, about your soul. You and your court spend too much time primping and beautifying your flesh, wearing lovely clothes and jewels to enhance your appearance, but none of you have come to me for confession, penance, and absolution. I can help you to beautify and adorn your souls, so that you may be welcomed into Heaven with loving arms by the glorious saints.

Lady Catherine stared at him with a blank expression as he spoke, although she arched an eyebrow every now and then. When he was done, she leaned across the table towards him, letting her long, strongly perfumed black hair fall forward. Keeping the same blank expression, she answered him:

Holy Father, I did not realize that you had made such strenuous efforts to notice the care I take to make myself beautiful, to ensure I am adored by all the lusting men around me. Are you falling into sinful thoughts? Are you having difficulty staying true to your vows? Perhaps you should find another priest to hear your confession. I worry your soul is getting soiled from my company.

Brother Nicholas did not enjoy being criticized—and, what was more galling, by a woman who had desecrated the holy communion host, and drank blood, and engaged in who knew what other filthy, demonic rites. How could she dare to cast aspersions upon others? Stifling his anger and disgust, he answered her as calmly as he could manage:

My Lady, we are all sinners. I too beg the forgiveness of my Father in Heaven for the wickedness inside me, for each time my eyes wander to the lures the Devil sets in my way. You must also do this hard labor of contrition, so necessary for your salvation. Reflect upon your sins, confess with a sincere heart, and you will find forgiveness and mercy in His infinite kindness and mercy.

Still leaning forward, Lady Catherine now smirked and returned to the attack: Wouldn't you agree that my soul's health only matters if my body dies? Because then I have no body, only a soul. But what if my body were eternal—then wouldn't it be more important to care for and tend to the immortal body? The soul would be merely an unwelcome nuisance in what you so lovingly described as my beautiful body—like a piece of rotted fruit giving me indigestion. Maybe I should expel my soul—empty it out of my anus into the privy.

Nonsense! You speak nonsense! he shouted at her.

Well, fine, she replied. Maybe you are right.

Lady Catherine leaned back in her chair now, and folded her hands in her lap. She closed her eyes for a minute, appearing to be in deep contemplation, before speaking again:

You keep telling me, Brother Nicholas, that I have grave sins to confess, that it will be such grueling labor to scrub my soul clean of them. But what are these sins? Can you tell me what my sins are?

Well, my Lady, we all have sins. We are born in sin.

She scrunched up her face in a playful manner and leaned forward again. He noticed now that she had painted her eyes with a bluish-black pigment that matched her thick hair and lent an intensity to her gaze. She said:

Come now, you can do better than that. You seem very, very worried about my sins. You care deeply about helping me to overcome them. If you are so sure I need to be confessed urgently, you must have some particular sin in mind— something more than simply having been born.

He was growing tired of being mocked by her. He decided it was best not to answer, but to stare sternly at her until her conscience made her feel ashamed of her conduct.

After a few moments silence, she spoke further: Well, let's examine some of the more important sins and see where I stand. We already talked about greed. As you heard, I am satisfied with what I have and seek no more. I leave my relatives and neighbors alone, and I don't steal from my peasants or the Church.

I am not a glutton. I try to eat well enough to keep in good health, but as you can see I eat only a modest portion of food.

I do not get angry. Even though you have been angry at me this evening, I have not been angry at you, no matter how often you accuse me of being a dreadful, unrepentant sinner.

What is next? Envy. I envy no one. I take pleasure in myself and do not covet what anyone else may have. I suppose that could sound like sinful pride. Perhaps that is my sin—I do feel happy that I am so beautiful, as you yourself can't help but notice.

No doubt you would charge me with sloth, but that would be false. I am quite industrious, just at nighttime instead of daytime. Thus I prefer to wake later in the day.

So that leaves lust. All you men of God love to talk about lust, it is your favorite sin—I am sure you prefer to hear confessions about lust rather than, say, someone envying the quality of his neighbor's horseshoes. With your painfully detailed observations about the lengths I go to be so ravishing, so desirable in my lithe form, you are certain, no doubt of it, that my soul is dirtied by lust and fornication.

But nothing could be further from the truth. I delight in being beautiful and being amongst other beautiful creatures and things, because beauty is pleasing and brings joy. But I have not lain with a man since my husband departed this world so many years ago—I have not even kissed another man.

I see from your face that you don't believe me, but do you know of any instance in which I have succumbed to lust? Can you name any lover of mine?

Brother Nicholas wracked his brain for a response, but he had none. While he had heard this estate was poverty stricken and remote, there had been no whiff of scandal. Indeed, it was the lack of such rumors that had led him to expect the lady of the castle to be a pious old woman. And for all their gross sacrilege, Lady Catherine's rites in the forest were chaste.

Feeling embarrassed now and unsure what to do, he looked down at his plate and focused on eating. After an awkward pause, one of the gallant, handsome youths suggested music to lighten up the sour mood. Her Ladyship readily agreed, and several maidens began to sing together in an impromptu chorus. Lady Catherine smiled broadly and clapped in time, encouraging her companions to get up and dance.

Brother Nicholas felt relieved to no longer be the butt of her mockery and abuse, and took advantage of the revelry to slip away. Lady Catherine nodded absently in his direction as he shuffled out through a side door.

IV. The Vampire's Confession

THE NEXT DAY, in the middle of the afternoon, a page came to the chapel to inform Brother Nicholas that he had been summoned to a private audience with Lady Catherine. He mutely obeyed, although not without some trepidation: he worried that he had been seen spying upon the black Mass and perhaps he would now be imprisoned, or his blood would be emptied into the wide bowl. On the other hand, his thoughts continued, perhaps she has a simple request of some sort. If she had wanted him killed or beaten, she could have easily sent a troop of her young men to do it.

When he entered her apartments, Lady Catherine was alone. She directed him to sit on one couch, while she sat down on an opposite one facing him. Then she began:

Good Brother Nicholas, I wish at last to make a full account of my sins. It has been many years since I last unburdened my soul to a priest. Will you hear my confession?

Of course. Please tell me, my Lady, what are your sins, and I will make sure you undertake the appropriate penance to cleanse your soul.

Nodding her approval of his words, she continued:

What are my sins? Well, you know some of them. Or you think you know some of them. But we must begin at the beginning. In the beginning, aren't we all born in sin? Yes, born in sin but then baptized. So what happened between my baptism as an infant and now to fill my soul with sins?

I was a good and pious child. I prayed to our Lord Jesus Christ and His Holy Mother each morning and each night. I was instructed by our family confessor, a kind old man with big round eyes and deep lines cut into his face, who seemed to see the next world more clearly than this one. He warned me against sin, and offered many examples from the lives of the saints and martyrs of how illusory and fleeting are the delights of this brief life and our physical bodies.

But in truth, and truth must be my watchword if this is to be a full confession, our family priest spent most of his time with the grownups. The man who truly did the most to make me a good Christian was my father. He was the lord of the castle where I grew up, and a mighty knight—tall, strong, handsome. Everyone yielded to him, and all the women stole secret greedy glances at him riding his horse in his glittering hauberk.

But I was special to him. While the other women, my mother, my aunt, the handmaidens, they could only stare and yearn, when I called to my father he would immediately come over. He would pick me up so we could ride together on that huge grey horse. The world would go by so swiftly around us, and the wind would whip my face and hair, and I would get scared, close my eyes, and say stop! Stop! And my father would laugh, hold me tight, and coax the horse to slow its pace. Eventually, I would be brave again and open my eyes and look up. And there he would be, smiling, confident, full of love for me. He would rub my hair and kiss my forehead. I felt so safe with him, and I was certain he was the strongest and bravest and best man in the world.

When the minstrels came to our castle, I would sit on his lap while they performed in the great hall. When they sang of heroes—of the knights of King Arthur's court, or of Charlemagne, or of mighty Tristan and his doomed passion for Isolde—I would always picture my father as the invincible hero—Lancelot or Gawain or Roland.

My father was always granting me little favors to the consternation of my mother. I was not allowed to have sweets during the day, but he would steal dried fruits and pastries from the kitchen and slip them to me. We were conspirators together against mother's awful tyranny of bland porridge and sour broth.

Or there was the time that I had to practice my dancing lessons, which I hated. I had such clumsy feet when I was a girl. I would trip over myself and make a mess of my clothes and all the grownup women around me—mother, aunt, my dancing teacher—would be so angry. One day, when they had furiously vented their rage upon me for falling and ripping my dress (it had caught on a peg), I ran away, out of the keep, out of the courtyard, and right past the gates. And there he was: my father. I knew him from his white armor and his white shield with the red dragon.

He took off his helmet, dismounted, and walked over to me. He went down on his knee, so that our eyes were level, and I just burst into tears and grabbed his neck. Why are you sad, my little Lady Catherine? he asked. And I told him how clumsy and stupid I had been and how I would never learn to dance, and mother had sworn no man would ever have me as his bride.

He replied to me, so softly: Your mother is just feeling upset. Her breakfast did not settle well in her tummy, that is all. You are a beautiful, courteous Christian lady. Any young knight would be more than lucky to be your groom.

Right then and there I loved him so much. I did not want any other man for my husband. I wanted him. I know that sounds foolish, but we are talking about the heart of a crying, trembling little girl.

But I am rambling. This is confession, and I need to focus upon my many sins. It was my father who made me a good Christian. He believed passionately in the goodness of our Lord Jesus Christ and the Holy Virgin Mother and the saints. He told me that if I had faith, and prayed genuinely with all my heart, God would protect me from evil.

In our family's chapel, there was a statue of Mary in a blue hooded dress, her face pale and gaunt, her eyes so big and sad. She feels everyone's suffering, my father told me, and she wishes the world were kinder.

I thought she was so wonderful. I wished she were my mother.

One day my father went to joust in a tournament. The meadow where they were going to fight was not far—less than a day's ride—but my mother absolutely forbade me to go. I begged and pleaded and sobbed and screamed, but she was adamant, no, that was not a place for a little girl.

My father told me not to worry, that he would not be gone long. He asked me for a piece of fabric from my sleeve, which I promptly ripped off for him. My mother looked annoyed, but we ignored her. I will tie this fabric to my helmet, he told me, just as each knight ties a ribbon from his beloved to his helmet. And if I, with God's help, come out victorious, I will not place the wreath of roses on the head of any pretty damsel there, but I will wait until I get home to crown you with it.

I hugged him and kissed his cheek. I was sure he was going to win. That night, I prayed so hard for his victory.

The next morning, he was off at the crack of dawn, before I was even awake. I waited anxiously all day. I prayed in the chapel. I wandered in the courtyard, and jumped in and out of the fountain. The hours went by so slowly.

At dusk, there was a great commotion at the gate. I ran over, sure it was my father with the wreath of roses for me. It was him, but there were no roses. He lay stretched out in a cart, screaming in pain. During the tournament his horse had lost its footing, and he had tumbled to the ground beneath the heavy mount. The bones in his legs and back had shattered in several places, and he could not move.

I tried to see him that night, but I was not allowed into his room. I was so scared, and no one would tell me what was happening. I went to the chapel and prayed to the Virgin Mother for my father, prayed harder than I ever had before. I remembered how full of love and compassion she was, and I knew, just knew, that she would help him.

The next day, as the sun began to set, I was finally able to sneak into my father's room. He lay asleep on his bed. The sight was horrible: his feet and calves were purple and green, and the skin was dried up, like dead leaves on the ground in autumn. I touched one of his green, withered toes—it was so cold—his warmth, that great warmth in him, had gone.

There were huge, whitish sores closer to the knees, and pus oozed out of them. It smelled so awful that I became dizzy, fell to the floor, and vomited. The noise of my retching brought my mother and the doctor into the room. She grabbed me by the hair and dragged me out. She told me to leave my father alone, and that if I wanted to help I should pray for him. And that is what I did, fervently and continually, for the next two days.

But the rot and decay continued to spread throughout his body. The doctors had recommended cutting off his legs and manly parts, but my mother refused—she would not be married to a cripple. My father's shame in living that way would be too great.

I have never felt such suffering as when I learned of my father's death. The priest, holding my mother's hand, told me to be strong and to be happy that my father was in Paradise, all his pain gone. If I were a good girl, I would join him there one day.

His words brought no comfort. I yelled at him: Liar! You're a liar! I prayed to God and His Holy Mother, and they didn't help him, he just got worse. You're a liar.

My mother struck me hard across the face, many times, telling me I was a horrible, wicked child, that my father had deserved so much better than me in a daughter, such a stupid, clumsy, selfish girl. Finally, the priest made her stop and I ran off. I went to the chapel, and banged my fists against the statue of the Holy Virgin Mother until I collapsed with exhaustion.

From that day forward, I have hated all mothers: I hated my earthly mother and I hated my heavenly mother.

As I grew into a woman, I kept to myself. The world felt strangely unreal to me without my father, as if I were trapped in a tree trunk and peeking out to watch someone else's life. I felt nothing—there was no sadness, but there was no joy either. I drifted along, like flotsam in a river, indifferent to what would happen to me. My mother would discuss marriage matches, but I would shrug. One is as good as another, I would say. Pick whomever you like.

It always went badly when I was taken to meet a prospective groom. He would praise my beauty and try to charm and impress me with his strength and his wit, but I didn't care and simply nodded along and waited for our meeting to end. His family would invariably reject me, appalled by my haughtiness and arrogance. My mother would scold me, too, and ask if I wanted to be a lonely old maid. But I merely shrugged.

After several of these ardent young men had really outdone themselves in praises for my beauty, I stood one afternoon in my room, alone, in front of a tall oval mirror. I stripped off my clothes, and I pulled the pins from my hair. I looked at myself naked: my skin pale and rosy at the same time, my wild unkempt hair running down to my waist and sticking out in strange jagged shapes.

Then I remembered my father, how his body had been so strong and beautiful before it was overrun by rot and decay. I tried to imagine my legs shriveling up and turning green, with pus-oozing sores all over, like his body had been at the end. I felt the inevitability of the fall of my flesh into rot, the loss of my beauty that was certain to come, an irrevocable sentence from the highest court in Heaven. My handsome young suitors would flee from me then.

I thought I would cry—I thought I should want to cry— but I did not. Instead, I found the idea that all the beauty around me was an illusion, which would dissolve into stinking pus and sores, to be quite a comfort. It reassured me that nothing mattered, and there was no good reason to care what happens in this life.

I now sought out the rot and decay in the world, so I could have fresh, visible proof of the futility of everything. There was a convent close to our castle, endowed by one of my ancestors. I went to the Abbess and asked her to let me serve the poor and the sick with the good nuns, to feed them and tend to them. She was overjoyed that such a noble young lady was interested in her holy work. My mother did not approve, but she could hardly punish me for doing what Christ had preached.

I started with the lepers. There was a small leper colony about a half day's ride from the convent. They were penned inside a circular stone wall. The nuns brought them food, clothes, and clean bedding two times a week.

When we entered, the lepers submissively lined up to receive our charity, although they were too ashamed to look us in the eye. Their faces were hideous, monstrous: rectangular pinkish bulges protruded all over their skin; many of them were missing all or part of their noses; and their eyes were clouded over—there were only blurry white ovals dotted with red spots.

One afternoon I asked an old leper woman if she was not, even slightly, angry at her Creator for her fate. No! she screamed. May He be blessed and bless us forevermore, He is all good, He is filled with love for me. I have brought this affliction upon myself. I sinned. I gave in to temptation. I deserve punishment. Let my soul be purified by my suffering in this false world, so that when I die He will welcome me to Paradise. He will take me to a place where there is no more pain, only love, love around me everywhere, because He is full of love for all His children.

And the other lepers also chimed in—they too were certain of God's love and goodness, and they too insisted that they alone were to blame for their afflictions—that this was only just penance for their many sins.

But what, I asked them, about the sinners who die fat and contented in their beds, healthy and intact? How can your punishment be just if they don't share it?

And the lepers replied: We are luckier than them, for we are doing our penance now, in this life. The others will be seared with purifying hellfire in Purgatory when they die, while we will go straight to Paradise.

Before I could ask them anything else, the nuns dragged me away, reproaching me bitterly for trying to shake the sincere faith of these simple souls. They accused me of sabotaging the lepers' salvation, of trying cruelly to extend their wretched suffering from this world into the next.

V. How the Vampire Made a Pact with the Devil

LADY CATHERINE CONTINUED her confession: After this incident, the Abbess shifted my duties from the lepers' colony to a house for fallen women, which the nuns maintained on the convent's estate. There were many women crammed together there, some carrying their former lovers' bastards, moaning from sickness or pain. I helped to tend and wash these women. I cleaned their vomit. I rubbed their sore, hideously swollen feet. I recoiled in disgust at their massive pregnant bellies with little creatures inside pawing and squirming about. And the sweat. Putrid, dank sweat all over their bloated bodies, which we could never fully wipe off.

There were also the sick women, whores who had contracted the great pox from their clients' diseased male organs. Their mouths and womanly parts were covered in grayish-white, oozing sores that we tried to clean. They had rashes on their feet and swelling in their glands. Large clumps of their hair fell out. These wretches had no future—who would ever touch, much less marry, such a revolting creature? But the nuns cared for them and urged them to repent, comforting them with a vision of the Paradise that awaited their souls if they truly confessed and gave their hearts wholeheartedly, with complete and loving faith, to Our Lord. And just like the lepers, the pox-infested women grasped on to their Heavenly Father as the one last being Who truly loved them—Who could love them tenderly and kindly, as no earthly man had ever done.

That is, with one exception. There was one girl, very young, who was afflicted with the great pox but refused to repent. You could tell she had once been very pretty, before her illness. She spat in the nuns' faces, and cursed her Creator and the foul lustful men who delighted in forcing their diseased, contaminated seed into every woman they found.

One afternoon I noticed this spiteful girl had disappeared. I asked the good sisters if something had happened—had her condition worsened, had she passed away from this life? The answer I received stunned me: the wicked girl, the nuns said, had simply walked off.

Prodded by both compassion and curiosity, I ordered our castle steward to send out messengers to find her and bring her back to me. When my mother protested, I reproached her for having no Christian pity for a sick unfortunate in desperate need of care and aid for both her body and her immortal soul. Our family confessor agreed, admonishing my mother about the need to fight for every soul's redemption. She was livid, and probably suspected I was up to something rotten. But she could do nothing about it.

Soon enough, the steward brought a pretty young girl to me, who claimed she had left the house of fallen women, but had no kin or husband to return to. When I saw her, I immediately recognized the impudent heretic, except that she had been completely cured of the pox—gone were all the sores and rashes, and her hair had grown back fully.

I took her for a walk in the castle gardens. I congratulated her on her recovery, and praised her restored beauty. How, I asked, had she been cured so quickly? Had she found a physician or an apothecary who had mixed a special potion? We should tell the sisters, I continued, they will be eager to know your secret.

The girl stopped walking and looked into my eyes. The nuns will be eager to know my secret, she repeated, in a dreamy, distant voice. And then she laughed—no, laugh is the wrong word. She cackled, like a mocking demon would cackle at a foolish sinner whom he had trapped. And there was a mischievous gleam in her eyes.

I don't understand, I said to her. Why are you laughing? This is a great miracle, a gift from God.

This only made her laugh more loudly. Once she had calmed down again, she looked at me quite seriously and asked if I wanted to know the truth about her cure. If I did, I had to swear that I would not tell the nuns—this particular secret, she said, was not for them.

I was confused, but I was too curious not to press on, so I gave her the oath she wanted.

Good, she said, the cure is simple: seek the aid of Lucifer, give yourself to him, and he will cure you. Frustrated that her prayers were being ignored, she had complained to the nuns of her Heavenly Father's indifference, if not outright cruelty, for an all-powerful, all-knowing, all-good being surely could and would cure her if He wanted to. The sisters had counseled humility, patience, and faith. They told her to focus upon her sins and how much she no doubt deserved her sufferings, lustful, vile sinner that she had been for so long.

But she did not consider herself to be a sinner. Her parents had both died shortly after she had blossomed into a woman, and with no other kin or husband, she had turned to a profession that gave her enough earnings to keep body and soul together with decent food and shelter—it was not her fault that she had been left alone, and certainly not her fault that men would deny her charity unless she first satisfied their filthy carnal appetites. So how could her diseased state, foisted upon her by one such fat-bellied man panting with his uncontrollable lust, be her sin?

She resolved to leave the nuns and to seek another way to heal herself. She ran away one night, far from the convent and deep into the forest. She kept running until she came across a thatched hut hidden behind a thick grove of old oak trees. Inside she found an old man, who took pity upon her. He heard her story and offered to help.

He lifted the coarse rug covering the floor of the hut to reveal a door, which he opened. He led her down a winding staircase into a large room where the white marble walls were dimly lit by torches. In this room, there were pews leading up to an altar. Behind the altar were stained glass panels, showing the most beautiful naked figures, one man and one woman. The old man explained that these were Adam and Eve, and their blinding beauty was how humanity was supposed to be, before we were cast out of the Garden of Eden, and cursed with hunger, disease, decay, and death.

Would you like to be cured, and be forever as beautiful as Eve? he asked.

How is that possible? she said. Our Lord in Heaven has rejected my prayers.

But, the old man said, there is more than one lord who can help you. Come, kneel before this altar.

And she did so.

He handed her a communion host but told her not to eat it. Instead, he explained, she must urinate upon it. Filled with resentment toward God, she happily did as he asked. Then he gave her something to drink, but she told me she nearly gagged because the liquid was so bitter and metallic. As she later learned, it was human blood.

Having administered this unusual sacrament, the old man told her to pray before the altar with all her heart and beseech the one who had built this place to cure her. As she prayed, an extraordinary light appeared and then faded to reveal a beautiful naked man, with blonde curls, pale blue eyes, and supple but slender muscles. He had immense white wings on his back. He bent over and whispered into her ear: I love you. I shall cherish and safeguard you as one of my daughters. Stand, and be healed.

Then the winged man disappeared. She felt her skin—the sores were gone. She felt her head, and her hair had grown back. She burst into tears and hugged the old man.

She stayed three more nights with the old man, taking her perverse communion with him each evening. On the third night, the winged man came to her in a dream. He said: If you do as I say, you will never be diseased again, and you will be young and beautiful forever.

What must I do? she asked.

You must kill a man and drink his blood. If you do not, the great pox will burst out again and overrun your body in sores and pus.

He told her there was a dagger in the old man's satchel lying near her on the floor. She was to take this dagger and slit his throat while he slept, and then slurp up his warm blood— as much of it as she could drink.

But isn't he your priest, your servant? she said. How can you betray him this way?

That is not your concern, the winged man replied. Make your choice: drink, and be healthy and beautiful, or fall back into disease, rot, and decay.

Suddenly, she woke up and saw the dagger in the old man's satchel sitting by her feet. She looked over and saw him snoring. Without thinking, she told me, like an animal hunting by instinct, she grabbed the dagger, cut his throat, and drank his blood.

But how can you stand here and confess such horrible crimes to me, without any guilt or shame? I asked her. Have you no worry for your immortal soul? Aren't you damned?

She laughed again, although this time more of a giggle. But I feel nothing, she said. And I am not damned, I am saved. Humanity was meant to be beautiful and young and immortal—that was how Adam and Eve were in the Garden of Eden. But then your Lord in Heaven threw them out and cursed them with sickness, death, old age and ugliness, just as he has kept cursing their descendants. Yet I have escaped the curse. I will never grow old and ugly, never rot or decay or die.

At this point, I ended our conversation and directed my steward to lock her in a room in our keep, although I made sure she was comfortable and well fed. I was not sure what to do. I knew I should denounce her at once—hand her over to the Church, tell them of her crimes, and let her be burned at the stake as she well deserved.

But I could not bear to condemn her. I recalled how terribly she had suffered from her loathsome disease, and how her many prayers had been ignored. She had certainly given Our Lord a fair opportunity to help her, but He seemed not to care. Still, the sisters would no doubt say her reward will come in the next life, not this one, in the eternal Paradise of Heaven.

Yet she had lost her faith in the rewards of Paradise. I mulled over why that could be—how could she care so little about the fate of her immortal soul. God judges your deeds in this life and then metes out just reward or punishment, or so I believed then. But she had stopped trusting in His judgment. Perhaps she reasoned that she could not trust a God who had ignored so many desperate, heartfelt pleas for relief from suffering. The only way to avoid falling into His power in the next life was to cheat Him of your death, to make sure your soul's ramparts—that is, the body encasing your soul—never rots or decays. Then your soul will stay down here, in this world, safe from the treachery of Heaven.

I thought of my father, how good a man he had been, how pious and honorable. Yet he was brutally taken from me, despite my prayers. I thought of the lepers and the diseased prostitutes, how they had been abandoned too. I was filled with such sadness and anger and confusion.

I decided I wanted to speak to this winged man, whatever he was, angel, demon, apparition. So the next night I ordered the girl to be freed and brought to me in the courtyard, where there were two saddled white mules ready for us. I dismissed the servants so we could be alone.

I want to meet him, I said, your winged protector. Take me to your secret altar in the woods.

She bowed her head slightly, said, Of course, My Lady, and mounted one of the mules. We rode out of the gate, past the nearby meadows, and into the forest. It was dark amongst the trees and I was worried we would become lost, but she knew the way, as if the path was paved and the light was bright.

We came to the hut and dismounted. When we entered, the darkness inside was so suffocating that I feared the girl had taken me there so she could kill me and drain my blood. I prayed silently and begged forgiveness for all my sins. It was the last truly Christian moment I had.

I heard a door creak open and a light burst forth from an opening in the middle of the floor. Relieved I could see again, I followed her down the stairs into an underground, dimly lit chamber. I saw the altar there exactly as she had described. She reached underneath it and handed me a communion host. If you wish to speak to him, she said, you must take his Eucharist. Defile this host with your urine.

And so I did.

Then she handed me a chalice of blood, and I drank from it.

At her direction I bowed my head and prayed, asking to speak to whoever watched over this place. The room went suddenly dark, and then I beheld the most glorious vision I had ever seen: a beautiful naked man, tall, blonde-haired, with spreading white wings and he smiled at me. There was such kindness in that smile.

He approached me and stroked my cheek. You are sad, he said. Would you like never to feel this sadness again?

I looked into his pale blue eyes—they looked like the most delicate spring sky—and I felt such warm love bathe my cold, shivering soul.

So without thinking, I said yes—please make my sadness go away.

The beautiful man said to me: From now on and forevermore, I will love you. There will be no more sadness for you. No old age, no disease, no suffering, no death; you will be young, lovely, and happy for eternity. In times to come, I will ask you to show that you return my love. But for now, rest and be at peace.

He cradled my head in his arms, like I was a little girl again in my father's lap, and I fell into a deep sleep. When I woke, I was at home in my own bed. The girl was gone and I never saw her again, although both mules had somehow returned to our stable.

I felt reborn, so full of energy, joy, and health—such incredible good health. The air felt invigorating in my lungs and the sounds of the birds filled me with delight.

I stopped assisting the nuns in their charitable work. I stopped going to Mass, too. The world was exploding with such life and color that I could not bear the glum, weeping statues in our chapel of the Holy Virgin and Child.

I summoned the finest tailors in all of Germany and had a whole new wardrobe of blindingly bright colors made for me—oranges and reds and yellows. I invited musicians to our court, and minstrels, and I asked other noble families to dine in our hall. My mother was overjoyed at this turn in my mood: she was certain my newfound gaiety and rosy complexion would land me a distinguished, wealthy husband.

And she was not wrong. For the first time, I was truly courted. Before I had been examined and prodded as a prospective bride, but without any enthusiasm from my would-be grooms. Now, however, they fell at my feet, reciting verses, declaring their eternal love, jostling each other to shout loudest of my peerless charms. I reveled in their attentions, and coyly encouraged each man to keep showering me with praise, even if I knew his cause was ultimately hopeless.

Every so often a man would fall too earnestly in love, and he would become embittered by my ways. These dreary spirits scolded me for being inconstant and loose—for not rewarding their devotions as they deserved. I made sure such dismal men were swiftly ejected from my presence. I had no tolerance for even the tiniest speck of malice or gloom.

Eventually I chose a husband, a young knight who was handsome, strong, charming, and of the finest noble birth— he was the last lord of this castle. We were married in the chapel here, and my wedding night was the happiest of my life.

I had not thought much about the winged man who had given me such abundant blessings. But when I fell asleep in my husband's arms on my wedding night, the winged man came to me in a dream.

He asked me if his blessings had brought me joy. I said yes and thanked him profusely from the depths of my heart. He smiled and stroked my hair. He then reminded me that I had promised to do what he asked to prove that I returned his love.

Anything, anything for you, I cooed, you have answered all my prayers.

Then, my daughter, he continued, you must kill your husband and drink his blood.

I woke with a fright. I stood up, walked to a window, and looked out at the stars hovering over the ramparts. I breathed heavily. I looked back at my handsome husband, snoring soundly. I told myself it was only a horrible, stupid dream.

Over the next month, my body began to change. I caught a chill and ran a fever. Sores cropped up on my face, throat, and chest, red and bulbous and leaking thick pus. Even though I recovered my strength, my sores would not heal—on the contrary, they spread further across my body. My skin burned, ached, and itched without respite. No matter what I did I was always uncomfortable. I looked at myself in the mirror, naked, and was horrified at the grotesque monster I had become. Filled with shame I covered myself with a thick veil, and avoided company, including my husband's.

The skin around my sores soon started to turn green and brittle, just like my father's skin had been in his last hours. I was terrified. My youth, my beauty, perhaps my life, were rotting away.

I had no other choice but to do what had to be done. I sent a note to my husband that I was well enough to visit his bed that night at midnight. When I entered his room, I dismissed the servants and bolted the door. I told him to close his eyes. I rubbed my silk dress over his naked body; he twitched with anticipation; he cried out that he loved me; he raised his lips to kiss me. I reached for the dagger I had hidden in my breast and slit his throat. As the blood gushed forth I lapped it up eagerly like a dog, trying to drink every drop. It was disgusting, bitter, metallic, but I forced as much of it down my throat as I could before I collapsed in exhaustion.

When I woke again, it was morning. My body was healed. I looked at myself in a mirror: I had never been so beautiful.

My husband's dead body had somehow disappeared from his bedroom. It was later found lying in the forest near this castle.

Rumors swirled. Because I was the last person with whom he had been seen, suspicion fell on me. I denied having a hand in his death—I said he had left me and gone out that night, that brigands must have killed him. I protested quite indignantly.

My husband's confessor demanded I swear on holy relics—the bones of a saintly hermit who had lived in these lands—that my account was true. I went to the chapel and put my hands on the hermit's skull, ready to swear to whatever they wanted to hear. Yet when my skin touched the sacred relics, my palms burned so terribly that I screamed out in pain and jumped away. I ran out of the chapel.

Then everyone abandoned me. The priest denounced me as a whore, a murderer, and a witch. The members of our household fled, including our knights. My husband's relations massed at the gates, armed and demanding my severed head in vengeance. I was alone with only a handful of servants and a small stock of food.

In my desperation I removed a communion host from the chapel, and defiled it. Then I cut my palm with a dagger and poured the blood into a wine cup, and drank it. Finally, I fell to my knees and prayed to the winged man—I did not even know his name, I just prayed to the memory of his image.

I swooned and fell to the ground, banging my head on the stone floor. But then I had a marvelous vision: I was in a garden in a valley beneath two vaulting peaks. A stream went by my feet. The winged man approached me and handed me six red roses. He was so handsome, with his blonde curls and his pale blue eyes. He asked me why I was afraid.

I told him my enemies had surrounded me, and that they were going to kill me.

Do not fear, he said, you have proven your faith and loyalty to me, and so I shall now prove my faith and loyalty to you. Your enemies will be turned back. Once they are dispersed, I will send you servants from my household, lovely and eternally young men and women, to wait upon you and to entertain you. They will summon my builders, who will beautify your castle.

As long as you continue to show your love and devotion to me, you will be forevermore beautiful, young, rich, and safe.

Then I woke from my stupor. I left the chapel and mounted the ramparts. Looking down on my enemies' tents outside the walls, I saw an amazing sight: their knights were packing up and running away, as fast as they could. And as they departed, they burned their camp and all its remaining stores and provisions. My husband's brothers and uncles rode after them, but the fleeing knights unsheathed their swords and cut my husband's family into pieces.

To this day, I do not know why my attackers scattered and fought amongst themselves. But every time, since then, when some armed band has approached these walls, lured by the castle's wealth, they have always turned on each other and burned their own supplies.

After my enemies had left my gates, I was visited by the same troop of lovely young men and women whom you have met. In all these years, they have never aged a day. I do not know if they are human or demon or something else, but they organized the household, recruited a full staff, and went out of their way to entertain and flatter me each evening.

Then came the builders, somber, gruff men. They hauled immense blocks of marble through these gates, more than I ever imagined existed in the world—more even than in the most decadent palaces in Cordova or Baghdad—and they erected the three extraordinary towers you see now. When they were finished, they left without saying a word of farewell. I ran after them, offering to pay, but they just laughed and kept going on their way.

Once the towers were built, the winged man came to me in a dream. He told me to perform the rites of his peculiar Mass each night. But where can I get the blood? I asked. He said in response: Obey me or forfeit my blessings.

Then he vanished. He has never spoken to me again. But I have taken his special sacrament each night, just as he demanded, and he has kept me beautiful, wealthy, and safe.

At first, I was not sure how to procure the necessary blood to drink. I shuddered at the thought of committing more murders. But then I thought matters over more closely. Everyone is cursed to die—Our Lord in Heaven saw to that when He cast us forth from Eden—and most peasants die long before reaching old age, from disease or a harsh winter or a poor harvest. So yes, I would be murdering them, but what did it matter if they would soon be dead anyway regardless of what I did?

Yet still I loathed the thought of doing the deed myself. I had so many nightmares about my husband's death—the way his body shook, the empty stare of his dead eyes, how quickly this powerful man with all his passions had turned into a thing lying about, like a broken old saddle in the corner of the stable.

So I asked my pretty handmaidens to hunt whatever men we needed for the blood for our special Eucharist. At night they would fan out from the castle into the countryside; they would lure men back here with the promise of exquisite pleasures of the flesh; and then, at some point during the act, they would cut their throats and drain the blood into wide bowls.

These beautiful young men and women have also tried to entice me into lying with them. There were times when I was sorely tempted. But I always refused them—I have been perfectly chaste since my husband's death. I remember too well the sight of the abandoned whores suffering from the great pox. Even worse was the thought of becoming pregnant. I have always been disgusted by a pregnant woman's body: that fat swollen belly, with the overgrown rodent inside kicking and scratching; and those fat swollen feet and hands.

I treasure the loveliness of my flesh—I delight in looking at it naked in the mirror, in running my hands on my soft skin and through my thick hair. I cannot bear the thought that some handsome youth's slimy seed will squirt into me and turn me into a sweating, panting, filthy, swollen pregnant monstrosity.

Now I have confessed all my sins to you. Or at least the important ones. But I don't want absolution. And I have no desire to change my ways. After all, what for? Your Heavenly Father has never answered my prayers, or the prayers of anyone else whom I have ever known. I have found someone better to pray to.

Although Brother Nicholas had sat quietly and patiently through Her Ladyship's long monologue, at this point he felt duty bound to interject: My Lady, you must repent. You have taken the first step, a great, courageous step—you have unburdened your heart in confession. You have been willing to take responsibility for terrible crimes—murder, heresy—but your soul must now be cleansed through penitence.

Lady Catherine reclined backward in her couch and sighed slightly. Then she spoke again, gently, in the tone of a wise old mother comforting an upset child: It has been a long time, my dear monk, since you believed the words that dribble out of the tight little corners of your mouth. You embraced the Church so wholeheartedly when you were young—wasn't she the temptress whose charms made you abandon your home and your family? Yet she has been so cruel to you. The Church broke your heart, poor thing. But I have a better way: Take my sacrament, and pray to my lord; he will bestow upon you also the blessings of everlasting beauty and youth and wealth.

I saw you creeping in the shadows at my midnight Mass in the forest. Why didn't you stop us? Jump out and demand we repent? Or go back to your Church and gather a force of the faithful to bring us to justice for our crimes? Isn't that what your Abbot or your Bishop would expect you to do?

At that moment Brother Nicholas wanted to flee, past the courtyard, past the gate, and far away from this woman. Yet he felt it would be wrong to leave—it would be cowardly.

But no, it was not a matter of bravery or fear. He realized, much to his chagrin, that he stayed there because he wanted to be near Lady Catherine—her voice, her hair, her eyes, her smell, they were all exerting some unsettling pull on his soul.

Nevertheless, he had to do what was right for her soul: My Lady, how can you speak so lightly of such rites, which require the murder of innocents? Can't you see how horrible and wicked it is to kill innocent souls?

Lady Catherine leaned forward and rested her chin on her fist. She assumed a thoughtful expression, and said: You are right, Brother Nicholas. For years, I told myself I was doing no harm in killing the men whose blood we drank. Everyone dies, most too soon, and I offered a quick and easy death in the arms of beautiful maidens—a death sweetened with intense pleasure. Much more pleasant than wasting away slowly from an awful disease in the corner of a moldy hut, surrounded by screaming children. Yet you are right, I could not avoid a nagging sense of guilt.

But I have now found a man who can give me blood endlessly without dying, or even weakening. And his blood is marvelous. Normal human blood is like bitter water mixed with tiny flecks of rusted iron. But this man's blood is sweet like honey. He has been touched by the divine, but left here to wander the Earth. Now that I have him to bleed, I can carry out my sacrament without harming anyone.

So to conclude this confession: I have nothing to repent. I am chaste and I harm no one, except this enchanted wanderer who always magically heals from any wound. So why should you inflict penitence upon me? I offer beauty and delight, without death or disease, and no one suffers.

VI. The Plight of the Wandering Jew

BROTHER NICHOLAS COULD not sleep that night. Lady Catherine had confessed herself to be an unrepentant heretic who had entered into a pact with some infernal power. Even though he had tried to lead her to the path of salvation, she had no concern for her eternal soul. He knew he should leave this place, denounce her, and let the Church's justice be done.

But he could not bring himself to do his duty. He recalled his past troubles, and how his brothers in the Church had viewed him with such suspicion. Even if they believed him— no, especially if they believed him—they would always suspect him of having had a hand in the wicked lady's devilry. It was the blood that would be the damning detail—so many of them were already convinced that, as a child, before he had embraced the true faith, he had no doubt partaken of hellish rituals involving baking human blood into *matzah*. Lies, he had told them so many times, wicked slanders against the Jews— slanders that were contrary to all the tenets of the laws of

Moses. Yet his fervent defense of the truth had only aroused rumblings that his baptism and conversion had been insincere.

Brother Nicholas's thoughts were suddenly interrupted, though, by a return of the loud, piercing screams that he had heard several nights before. This moaning was not human; no man could cry out so loudly for so long—if a man were in such pain, he would have lost consciousness soon enough. Yet whoever this sufferer was not only stayed conscious and alert through his ordeal, but he maintained the strength in his lungs and throat to vent his unhappiness across the whole castle.

With his temples throbbing from the terrible screams, Brother Nicholas dressed quickly and left his rooms for the courtyard outside. He followed the sound to a window looking into one of the towers. Through this window, he saw two clothed maidens standing beside the same naked, bearded man chained to a cross whom he had seen on his first night in the castle. As on that earlier night, one woman pierced his ribcage with a spear while the other gathered the gushing blood in a wide bowl. And as before, no one else in the castle seemed to notice or care that there was such awful suffering in their midst.

But this time no one assaulted Brother Nicholas as he watched the scene unfold. Once the bowl was full, the maidens put the spear away in a locked chest and left with the blood they had gathered.

After watching the two maidens leave the room, he turned his eyes back to the naked prisoner, whose wounds had somehow already completely healed. The man now appeared to be strangely calm and even comfortable. He looked at the floor, and made odd, playful faces. Eventually he looked up and stared directly back into Brother Nicholas's eyes just outside the window. The prisoner nodded and smiled in a friendly way, as if they were passing each other on the road to a country fair.

Brother Nicholas felt a rush of terror and had an impulse to flee, but he was also curious who this man could be and how he could so easily endure such torture. He walked around the edge of the tower, feeling its outer wall carefully in the heavy darkness, until he found a door. He pushed lightly, and it gave way.

He walked towards a dim light shining from somewhere inside the tower, leaning a hand against the wall to keep his balance. He felt himself descending a wide stone staircase. The light grew brighter as he went on and, at the bottom of the steps he found a large, partially lit candelabrum resting on a table.

Beyond this table was another door, which had been left open. Brother Nicholas took the candelabrum and went inside, and there he found the naked, bearded man strapped onto the cross.

He placed the light on the floor. The prisoner looked at him with a blank expression and sighed. Brother Nicholas stood in silence for several minutes, unsure what to do.

Finally, he spoke: What is your name, friend?

I go by Cartaphilus, the man replied. His voice was both relaxed and booming, as if, Brother Nicholas reflected, he was in perfect health, the robust lord of the castle riding out on an early morning boar hunt.

My new friend, Cartaphilus, I give you greetings in the name of our Savior and His Holy Virgin Mother. I am Brother

Nicholas. Are you hurt? I saw them puncture your ribs, and you lost so much blood, but I cannot see now where your wounds are.

Cartaphilus sighed again. His face assumed an expression of impatient exhaustion, as if he was being asked to undertake the same tedious task yet again.

It is a pleasure to make your acquaintance, monk. It would indeed be a blessing if I actually could be wounded. It would be an even greater blessing if one deep wound could sever my body from my soul. But my soul is trapped and imprisoned in this body, which is, for the time being, indestructible. I have prayed many times to the Holy One, Blessed be He, for the sweet release of death, but my prayers do not seem to reach the Throne of Glory.

Brother Nicholas recognized that phrase, the Holy One, Blessed be He—it was *HaKodesh Borech Hu*, the ancient rabbis' name for the Heavenly Father. Brother Nicholas looked more closely at the naked Cartaphilus and saw as well that he was circumcised.

Are you a Jew? Brother Nicholas asked.

Cartaphilus smiled. I suppose I am, or I suppose I was. I am alone now—my fellow Jews do not welcome me into their company anymore. If I tell them my tale, even though every word I speak is the truth, they curse me as a liar or a madman and drive me away. Sometimes I pretend to be a beggar so I can stay with the paupers in the back corner of a synagogue and hear the sounds of the Torah chanted in Hebrew. In my long years of wandering I have learned many languages, like yours, but they all sound to me like metal banging or a man vomiting up his supper. Only Hebrew has ever sounded truly lovely to my ears.

Will you tell me your tale, friend? Perhaps I can find a way to help you.

Cartaphilus laughed. It is tiring to repeat the same tale so many times, over and over through the decades and the centuries. And no one cares for my story. Both Jews and Christians feel mocked and insulted by my words, even though my words are true. So they send me away and try to forget the uncomfortable parable that is my life. Although, I should not complain so bitterly. Perhaps the point of it all is to spread my tale and hope it can serve as a lesson—although I am not sure what lesson I am teaching.

And perhaps the repetition keeps my memories fresh and vivid.

But I suppose you want to hear it, don't you, Monk?

Brother Nicholas said he would, very much so.

Do you swear, Monk, by whatever it is you take sacred and binding oaths upon, that you will leave me in peace no matter what I tell you?

Of course, he answered, if you tell me of crimes and sins, I will consider this to be holy confession, and the confession to be for the sake of contrition and penitence.

Cartaphilus nodded, inhaled deeply, and began:

I always start my tale the same way, at the beginning. The story has no end, but it does have a beginning. That beginning was long ago, in Jerusalem, where I was born in the last years of the reign of King Herod. My family were cobblers, as far back as anyone could recall—perhaps when my ancestors had returned from exile in Babylon, they made shoes for Ezra and Nehemiah, may the memory of the righteous be for a blessing.

We lived close to the Temple, and like many people in Jerusalem then, we made our living from the pilgrims who came to offer sacrifices and prayers. They would wear away their shoes on their long journeys from Parthia or Egypt or Italy or wherever. We would repair them and resole them, or sometimes sell new shoes if the old ones were too damaged. It was a good living, although it had its drawbacks. The noise from the Temple—people arguing, animals screeching out as they were killed on the altar—could be deafening, and some days I had to walk away beyond the city walls, into the hills, to calm the pounding in my head.

When I grew to be a man, I also became a cobbler. I married a sweet and shy girl and we had five children, three daughters and two sons. We lived in my father's old shop, which I had inherited when he died. We had our little ups and downs, and little was the right word for them: the scale of my life was mercifully little back then. I assumed I would live and die on that back street near the holy Temple, mending shoes until my hands were too old and arthritic to keep working.

And then I was cursed. It happened one afternoon during *Pesach*. Because the Romans feared that the Jews might take rebellious inspiration from the tale of the Exodus from Egypt and the liberation from bondage, they always made a point of crucifying troublemakers during *Pesach*. That afternoon Roman soldiers were leading a group of convicted criminals to Golgotha, a hill just beyond the Jerusalem city walls, where they would all be crucified.

I went outside my shop to watch. The wretches were dragging their huge wooden crosses on their shoulders, moaning in pain. The Roman soldiers looked bored. They were sweating miserably under their gear and cursing in Latin under their breaths. They whipped the prisoners to move faster.

I was also impatient for the criminals to get out of the city and up on their crosses. No one was going to enter my shop as long as they were marching along the street in front of me.

And then one man, bearing a cross on his shoulder, stopped right in front of me. He was short and fat and his flimsy tunic was soaked through with sweat. He smelled awful. He looked at me and scratched his beard. I looked back at him and waited for him to move on. And I waited some more. But he just stood there. A Roman soldier yelled at him, but he did not seem to care.

Then came the fateful moment when I was cursed, a curse which has lasted now for hundreds of years. It all happened so fast—isn't it strange how hard it is to recognize the truly important events right when they happen to you? He asked me: Can I have a drink of wine and rest my shoulders against your wall? But I was so annoyed at the amount of time it was taking him and his fellow convicts to walk past my street that, without even thinking, I screamed at him to hurry up and get out of my sight.

To be honest, it felt good to yell at someone at that moment.

The little fat man looked deeply offended—affronted, actually, yes he appeared indignant and affronted at my words, as if I were a guest in his house who had just urinated on his tablecloth. He said to me: Since you have not let me rest today, you are cursed never to rest until the end of time. And then he picked up his cross, and he was back on his way to Golgotha.

Surprised at the fat man's behavior—convicts under the lash of the whip are usually not so haughty—I asked my neighbors who he was. They told me his name was Yehoshua ben Yosef. The family were carpenters, decent folk, but then Yeshua—that was what they called him—decided he had been uniquely anointed by the Holy One, Blessed be He, for some great mission. He acquired a small band of followers and drew just enough attention to himself to make it worthwhile for the Romans to include him in the roundup of agitators.

I did not take Yeshua's curse too seriously. Jerusalem was filled with madmen who thought they were prophets or messiahs. This one, this Yeshua, had an angry mother, who about a week later barged into my shop to scold me for having been so cruel to her son. Her name was Miriam. She was a bald and wrinkled crone, all skin, bones, and rage. I tossed her back outside without a second thought.

So I forgot about the curse from this Yeshua and went on with my life. But after a couple of years, I began to notice certain things, unusual things. I had stopped ageing. No more wrinkles or grey hairs grew upon my head. And I had stopped getting sick. Even when everyone else in my house or my street was afflicted with some illness, I remained in perfect health.

And then something happened that made clear the curse was real. There was a runaway horse in Jerusalem, bounding fast through the narrow streets, so fast I did not see it. I walked right in front of this horse, which knocked me down onto the cobblestones and trampled me under its hooves. I should have been dead or crippled. Or at least hurt. But once the horse had gone away, I stood up, wiped the dust off of my tunic, and felt fine.

A crowd of people surrounded me, marveling at how I had survived such a calamity without a scratch. Someone screamed I must be a demon, and charged at me with a dagger. In my stunned state I moved too slowly, and my attacker drove a knife into my belly. But again, I felt no pain, more a mild discomfort—as if I had a hair caught in my mouth and wanted to get it out. I pulled the knife out of my stomach and handed it back to the man.

Everyone now ran away from me in terror. When my wife and children heard what had happened, they too were terrified and begged me to explain how I had performed these wonders. But I could not explain what had happened.

My wife and my sons took me to the priests at the Temple. They instructed us to make this offering and that sacrifice, but it did no good: afterward I would prick my palm with a sharp knife, and there would still be no pain.

Baffled and frustrated, I left Jerusalem and wandered westward, toward the coast. Near a sandy beach, on a small hill, I found a modest temple built by the Gentiles for one of their idols. When I entered, I saw a green marble statue of a beautiful woman and a priestess in a plain white dress who was burning incense on an altar.

She turned to look at me. What ails you? she asked. Perhaps Isis can soothe your troubles.

I cannot die or be wounded, I replied. My family, my neighbors, they all think I am some kind of demon.

She took my hand, and we kneeled down together to pray to her idol—a horrible sin, I know, but I was lost and despairing, and the priests of the One True Living God had failed to help me. There was a thunderclap and then a bright light. The priestess looked at me again, but her eyeballs were now entirely white. She seized my cheeks, she felt all over my head with her hands, and then she kissed my lips—but not with love, no, this was a feral kiss, as if she were trying to suck something out of my gut and into her mouth.

When she had finished and her eyes had returned to their normal color, she looked at me with such pity. She said: A god has cursed you. He asked your aid and you spurned him, so you are cursed never to rest. You will wander forevermore, with your soul trapped in a never ageing, never dying body. Even Isis cannot help you.

Now I understood: Yeshua had been no arrogant false prophet, he was a god. And I was cursed. So I sought out his followers, told them my tale, and asked them if they could help me. But they mocked me and smacked their lips with malicious glee. They clearly believed I had been given the punishment I deserved.

I decided to leave my family, so they could live out their allotted days free from my curse. I sailed far away to Valentia in Hispania, which was then also ruled by Rome. There I took up my trade as a cobbler. I refused to speak of my past other than to say I was a Jew who had been forced to flee from my home.

After a time, when the questions about my past had died down, I was offered several marriage matches by the local Jews. But I rejected them all: lonely as I was, I could not inflict my curse on another. Instead, I sought solace in the brothels. I would spend wildly in the houses of ill repute, on drink, on women, losing myself in the happy oblivion of tipsy pleasures. And why not? I had no family to support with my wages, and I had no need to save money for my old age, because I cannot age.

Still, word of great events eventually wound its way to me, even if I did not want to hear it. The Temple in Jerusalem was destroyed. I tried to imagine what had happened to my sons, and to my wife if she were still alive; I could see in my mind the Roman soldiers beating them, killing them, burning our house and shop. To wash away these thoughts, I drank even more wine, and I threw even more coins to the prostitutes to embrace me tightly.

Yeshua's followers were growing rapidly. In Hispania, they called him by his Latin name, Jesus. The Emperor, who no longer lived in Rome but in a new capital, Constantinople, became a follower of Yeshua and credited his victories to Yeshua's blessing. The Emperor's mother even wandered about the hills around Jerusalem trying to find pieces of Yeshua's true cross.

Churches sprouted everywhere like weeds. Eventually, a little more than three hundred years after I had been cursed by Yeshua, I wandered into one of these churches. It was quite solemn: the Mass was sung in a melancholy, lilting tone, and the congregants mutely received their sacrament with head bent and eyes cast down. I walked along a side wall, observing the worshippers, until I came to a statue: a tall, willowy man in a white tunic, with long wavy brown hair and beard, a truly lovely man; and next to him, holding his hand, was an even lovelier woman, with long black hair and sad blue eyes. I bent over towards a young man, who was clearly quite devout, and asked him to tell me about the statues.

He said: That is Our Lord Jesus Christ, Who died so that we may live, and His Holy Virgin Mother, Mary.

I looked back over to the statues. I remembered the fat, sweaty Yeshua who cursed me and his bald, nagging crone of a mother Miriam, and then I laughed. But not quietly: I roared with laughter. The service abruptly stopped and everyone stared at me as I kept laughing, oblivious to their indignant dour faces. Eventually, the priest gestured to two burly men who grabbed me, hauled me out of the church, and brought me to the villa of the local Bishop.

Once the Bishop had heard what had happened, he demanded I explain why I had so rudely interrupted the church services and what was the meaning of my laughter. I spoke the truth to him: how I had been a cobbler in Jerusalem, how I had been cursed to eternal wandering by his Jesus, and how Jesus' followers had no inkling what their savior had actually looked like when He walked the Earth.

After hearing my story, the Bishop said: If you are being truthful, would you let my guard plunge his sword in your belly?

I shrugged my shoulders and sighed with boredom— eternity makes everything faintly ridiculous and tedious.

Glaring with rage, he ordered his guards to run me through. I stood there, quite still, while they hacked at my body with their swords. When they had exhausted themselves and stepped away from me again, I had no wounds.

The Bishop crossed himself. He screamed that I was a demon. He babbled exorcism spells. But I simply stood there, waiting for this overexcited man to calm down. At last, he ordered that I be taken to the local Jewish community.

Over the centuries, I had drifted apart from the local Jews. But now, for one glorious night, I again shared their food and wine and fellowship. They cursed the Bishop and the Roman governor, and spoke longingly of how one day the *Mashiach* would come and restore the Temple in Jerusalem.

Matters took a turn for the worse the next morning. The Jews asked me how I had so deeply offended the Bishop. And I told them my tale, just as I told him and just as I told you. Then they exploded with rage: I was a demon! What other explanation could there be? Jesus was an imposter to them— a fraud, a son of a harlot, a heretic who had betrayed his own people and now rightfully smoldered in *gehenna*. How could such a vile man, who was merely a man, have had the power to unleash such a terrible curse? So I must be lying. Demons are deceivers, and demons would also be impervious to harm from human weapons.

I was thus shunned by both the Jews and the Christians. Seeing no place for myself anymore in Valentia, I left one morning by foot on the main road. Over the years, I made my way through Hispania, across the Pyrenees, and into Gaul, and from Gaul to Germany.

I eventually came to the lands of the Lady Catherine. Everything was so desolate here. The trees were stunted, their fruit small and bitter; the fields were overrun with weeds and skeletal brown mice; the livestock were gaunt and wobbly; and the few people about were even thinner and weaker.

I went into an inn. I asked the innkeeper what had happened—had there been a plague? Had invaders laid waste to the countryside?

We are cursed, he said to me, cursed and damned ever since our true lord, may his soul rest in peace, was murdered. His widow, the lady of the castle, is an ungodly woman; she worships the Devil—she has made some kind of pact with the Devil so that she can live in luxury and safety within her walls while we suffer in this land where everything withers and dies.

How can she survive, I asked, if her lands are so impoverished?

The innkeeper looked to his left and to his right before responding, and then crouched close to me and whispered: Because she does not live on food. She lives on blood. People have told me that they have seen her and her followers drinking blood in the forest. And they get the blood by luring the few men left here into sin. She sends out these demons in the guise of beautiful women, who lure men away at night into the castle, and then they are never seen again. Sometimes their corpses are found weeks, or months, later, totally drained of all the blood.

The innkeeper advised me to stay indoors that night, in his rooms, and then leave this place at the first light of dawn.

But I was too excited by the novelty of alluring demon women. The years of wandering had been quite monotonous, fields and villages and churches that look so alike wherever I go. And I thought, perhaps these demon women, if they are truly demons, can kill me and lift my curse so my soul can finally rest in the World to Come?

So that night I wandered in the woods beneath a bright moon, singing loudly and joyfully to attract their attention. And soon enough, there they were: two beautiful maidens in tight-fitting gowns who strolled about easily and confidently in the night. They greeted me sweetly, and each maiden took one of my arms. They launched into wild flatteries about how handsome I was, and they moaned pitiably about how lonely they were. I enjoyed their performance and let them lead me into the castle.

They brought me into this room. They undressed and began to lie with me, but while they did so, they discreetly bound my hands and my feet. Then I saw a dagger flash in the reflected moonlight and felt it plunge into my neck. I screamed—I was surprised that it hurt so much. They drained my blood into a bowl.

They stood up when they were finished. I then asked that, if they needed no more blood, could they please untie me. Their faces turned pale when they saw me still alive and without a wound—after all, until that moment, they must have thought I was an ordinary lustful man like any other. Off they ran, and it was their turn to scream.

Shortly after sunrise, they returned and released me. I spent a pleasant morning exploring the castle grounds and marveling at the great wealth of these towers, so opulent even though the countryside is so poor. Perhaps it is the Evil One's power of illusion.

At dusk, I was taken to Lady Catherine's apartments. She kept her distance from me—she would recoil violently every time I lurched close toward her body—but she was kind and welcoming. She apologized for the behavior of her ladies in waiting, whom she said could get overexcited. She asked me how I could survive being stabbed in the neck. So I told her: I had been cursed to wander eternally, so nothing could harm me.

But what happens when you lose your blood, she asked me, don't you get weak? Light headed?

No, I replied. It is replenished as soon as it is lost.

So, she pressed on, you can be pricked, stabbed, beaten, bled out, again and again and again, but you will always heal and continue to wander this Earth? That is your curse?

That is my curse, I said. My soul cannot be released from the prison of this body to find rest in the World to Come.

I had a pleasant dinner with her Ladyship that night, but when I drank the sweet brandy afterwards, everything went dark and I collapsed upon the table. When I awoke, I was back in this room, chained to this cross. The two maidens, both so lovely, still visit me to take my blood. But they no longer make the effort to flatter me, or even to speak. They are as solemn now as a priest at Mass. One of them thrusts the spear into my ribs; the pain is searing, I feel lightheaded, nauseated, and I cannot help myself but to scream. But it is not so bad: they cannot actually hurt me, and there is something wondrous about the pain—it breaks the tedium.

So now you know who I am, Monk, and why I heal so miraculously. I am surprised at how calm you are. Most of your brothers would have already erupted in fury against me. After all, I have told you, Monk, how your god of love had acted so cruelly towards me on such a slight pretext. Don't you care to protect His honor and good name? You are not much of a credit to your Holy Church.

Brother Nicholas felt embarrassed at this rebuke. He should have become angry at this man. But he felt an affinity for this eternal wanderer in his loneliness, spurned by both Jew and Christian alike. Still, he should think of a proper chastisement for Cartaphilus's mocking words.

Yet while he struggled to summon an appropriately indignant response, Brother Nicholas found himself imagining Cartaphilus long ago and far away in the Temple courtyard in Jerusalem, in a purple twilight, as the priests and the Levites were cleaning up the blood and innards from the day's many animal sacrifices.

And then an old, fuzzy memory from his distant childhood bubbled up to the forefront of his mind: the Garmu family, the secretive dynasty of bakers who alone knew how to bake the shewbread required for the Temple in Jerusalem. He had read it in … where had he read it? … Not in Latin … Yes, he had read it in Tractate Yoma. One of the Talmud's marvelous digressions into what life had been like when the Temple stood, before the Jews' many sins had brought the yoke of the Exile down upon their heads.

So instead of sternly reprimanding Cartaphilus, Brother Nicholas suddenly blurted out, like an excited schoolboy: Did you know the Garmu family? When the Temple stood, did they bake the shewbread? What were the loaves like? Why could no other baker bake it?

Cartaphilus looked surprised and confused. After a brief pause, he asked how a Christian monk would know about the Garmu family of bakers—such history was not recorded in the Christian books in Latin and Greek, as far as he knew.

I was born a Jew, Brother Nicholas replied, and it was only when I grew older that I saw the light of the Church's teachings. But your story reminded me of a passage in the Talmud I had once read as a boy. My father was a baker, and I liked to imagine he was somehow a member of the Garmu family.

Cartaphilus's face now assumed a terrible cast. Breathing heavily and pulling against his chains, he thundered at Brother Nicholas: You are an abomination! How can you abandon your people Israel, in the midst of their terrible Exile, to follow this false god, to bow to His idols and His mother's idols in their churches? And not only did you betray the one true Master of the Universe, the Holy One, Blessed be He, but you became a priest for their foul rites? You spread their lies willingly, actively?

Many times the Christians have tried to persuade me to join them, to put my head in their baptismal fonts. They say to me, Your people, the Jews, have spurned you because you are living proof of the great power and divinity of Our Lord Jesus Christ. Accept Him into your heart as your Savior, have faith in His gospel, and He will surely lift your curse. Love Him, bow down to Him, and He will love you in turn and end your sufferings.

But I have never heeded these lies. Although my fellow Jews may revile me for now, I will not betray them. When Joseph was betrayed by his brothers, were they not still one family? Were they not ultimately reconciled to one another? So it will be with me: I shall, one day, be reconciled with my brothers again, even if I must wait for the coming of the *Mashiach*, may it be speedily and in your days.

You were born a Jew, so you have heard the words of the holy Torah. Do you recall the words of *Sefer Devarim*, from the weekly portion *Ha'Azinu*? When Israel sacrificed to demons and false gods, the Holy One, Blessed be He, hid His countenance from them, and His arrows were drunk with the blood of the Israelites who had betrayed Him.

And look where you have ended up, idol worshipper. I am sure you too are a doomed prisoner in this castle. How long before the maidens finish arousing your lusts and decide to drain your blood? Only you will not survive. Your soul will be cast into the pits to be tortured with all of the rest of Israel's idol worshippers. Ashmedai's demon servants will melt down the golden calf before your eyes and pour the bitter, scalding gold dust down your throat.

Cartaphilus then spat three times on the ground.

Brother Nicholas felt unable to speak or move. Cartaphilus's words had wounded him, even though he told himself to disregard them as lies. Maybe the wanderer is a demon, he thought, sent by Lucifer to walk the Earth and lead good Christians astray. If Brother Nicholas still considered himself to be a good Christian.

Eventually, he mustered the strength to shuffle silently out of the room, eyes cast down to evade Cartaphilus's angry glare.

VII. The Jewish Monk

BROTHER NICHOLAS HAD first felt the stirrings of his Christian faith when he was twelve years old. It had happened on a Saturday afternoon. The lord who owned the town where his family lived had been unwell. The lord's estranged wife, who had fled far away to her family's lands, had recently died. According to the rumors that spread about, the lord was now racked with guilt about the coarse peasant mistresses he had kept in her place and the litter of bastards he had sired. Under the guidance of his previously neglected confessor, he turned to prayer, contrition, and the generous endowment of monasteries. And as a further part of his penance, he ordered his Jews—including Brother Nicholas's family—to assemble in the town's church on that Saturday afternoon so that a local priest could preach the true Gospel to them and urge them to accept baptism.

The town's Jews were upset at this decree, but what could they do? Their homes and livelihoods depended upon their lord's goodwill. For many years he had left them in peace, too busy fornicating, drinking, and hunting to care about them. Perhaps, the Jews whispered to each other, this newfound zeal is just a passing fancy. We will humor him and sit in his church and listen politely to the priest's silly nonsense.

Yet when the time came, the short walk to the church proved hard. The Jews spoke not a word to one another as they filed awkwardly and haltingly into the pews, beneath the glaring, disapproving eyes of a tall statue of some Christian saint.

Yossele (as Brother Nicholas was then known) sat with his *tate*, who held his hand tightly. He had never been inside a church before. It was the tallest building he had ever seen—his eyes could barely make out the stone arches on the high ceiling. There was an immense altar in front of the pews and behind it rectangular panels of stained glass lit up by the afternoon sun.

The stained glass pictures were full of bright, vivid colors, much more intense than anything Yossele had ever seen before. There was a gaunt man nailed to a wooden cross with a crown of thorns upon his head and his ribs protruding from his chest. His eyes, filled with such pitiable suffering, looked out at the silent, tense Jews in the pews. Next to him was a woman weeping. Her face was pretty, and her skin was unblemished and blindingly white, so different from the dirty, wrinkled faces of the women Yossele saw in his father's bakery shop.

A plump, self-assured Christian priest confidently strode up to the lectern and looked out at the assembled Jews, who averted their eyes from him. After a moment of silence, this priest then launched into his sermon. He spoke of how the

Jews had betrayed their covenant with God and were now scattered and dispersed, reduced to powerlessness and exile as a righteous punishment for their many and terrible sins. He thundered that they had betrayed and murdered their savior Jesus, and they must now repent.

Tate squeezed Yossele's hand ever more tightly. Yossele offered a silent prayer for this ordeal to end—the anger from the priest, the anger from his *tate*, he wanted it all to go away; he wished he were back in his home.

But then something happened that he had not expected. The priest dropped the rage and disgust from his voice, and now spoke gently, sweetly even. He described Jesus' love for the poor, and the miracles he had worked. He told of a leper, a decent man who had lost his livelihood and friends because of his boils and sores. The sickness had spread to his eyes, so that he could barely see anymore. The priest described how this leper had staggered about half-blind in his torn rags, begging for scraps of food and shivering wretchedly in the dark alleyways at night.

And then this leper, who had been shunned by everyone, even his own family, knelt down before Jesus, who kissed him, cured him, and offered him God's love.

Yossele was deeply moved. He started to cry, but then he caught his father's pulsating, raging glare. His compassion instantly turned to guilt. He felt that he had betrayed his *tate*, although he told himself there was nothing wrong with pitying the poor leper's sufferings.

The priest continued: Jesus had a far more important mission than merely succoring the downtrodden. His task on Earth was to undo the terrible calamity that had happened at the dawn of creation, when Adam and Eve's sin had forced all their descendants to be banished from Paradise. Jesus would take the guilt of that sin, and of all the many sins committed since then, upon himself alone, so that humanity could once more ascend to Heaven.

The priest said that the Jews of Jesus' time were cruel. He spoke of how the Temple priests in Jerusalem, corrupt and greedy, exploited the poor and were furious with Jesus for coming to their aid. They had him arrested, beaten, publicly humiliated, and nailed to the cross, to die a miserable death in the burning dry sun, with the birds nibbling at his eyes and a Roman lance thrust into his ribcage. Yossele looked again at the stained glass, at the man on the cross with his agonized gaze. He felt sorry for him.

Back at home that evening, as *mame* lit the *Havdalah* candle to mark the end of the Sabbath, everyone was quiet—it was like when Yossele's *bubbe* had died and there was a tense silence among all the adults. He felt that his parents were bursting with stifled hatred, and that somehow he was disappointing them and failing them by not sharing in their anger.

That night, Yossele dreamed about Jesus, who looked just like the image in the stained glass. Jesus stroked his cheek and told him that God loved him. But then wicked men dragged Jesus away. Yossele cried out in his sleep, and woke in a panicked sweat. His mother came to him, and asked what had frightened him so. He lied, and said he had forgotten his dream.

He had this same dream each night for the next two weeks. These dreams of Jesus became his dirty, shameful secret. This shouldn't be so, he told himself, the Jesus of his dreams was kind and warm and good. But he knew that this was something that could not be spoken of.

One day at twilight, after *cheder* had ended, but before his absence from home would be noticed, he snuck back into the church. It looked empty, and a chilly draught was blowing through the pews. But the pink light of the setting sun lit up the stained glass, and there was Jesus again, with his pained, imploring expression and crown of thorns. Yossele ran through the aisle between the pews, past the altar, and right up to the stained glass. There he knelt down in front of the picture of Jesus on the cross. His body trembled, and his eyes moistened, but he felt a deep calm and sense of joy for the first time since the dreams had begun.

Eventually a priest knelt down next to Yossele—a different priest than the fat man who had preached to the town's Jews. This priest was wrinkled, bald, and raggedly thin. He softly asked Yossele what had brought a Jewish boy to the church at this hour. Yossele looked up at his warm brown eyes and confessed everything about his dreams—everything he had been hiding from everyone else.

Would you like to know more about Jesus' teachings and miracles? the priest asked. Yossele said yes, he would. So they arranged that three times a week, in the very early morning, he would come to see the priest and learn Christian ways, their teachings, their stories, even their Latin language, which confusingly read left to right, instead of the right to left he had been accustomed to all his life from the Hebrew letters.

These secret lessons continued for several weeks. Yossele felt he was living an outer, lying life as a pretend Jew, and an inner true life as a Christian. Sometimes this tension would exhaust him, terrified as he was of being exposed as a traitor to his fellow Jews. But there was also something exciting about his secret Christian study: he felt superior to the Jews around him, because he—and none of them—possessed the searing truths of Jesus' revelations. Still, at that time he could not yet imagine actually abandoning his parents and living openly as a Christian.

Despite his best efforts at concealment, Yossele was found out. One late Friday afternoon, after he had helped his family close the bakery shop for the Sabbath, his father suddenly grabbed his arm and dragged him past the synagogue and the *cheder* to the rabbi's house, where it seemed all the Jewish fathers in the town had assembled.

They shoved him down into a hard wooden seat. The rabbi approached, a squat bulldog of a man with an immense black beard. What is your business at the church? he demanded of Yossele. You have been seen entering and leaving several times. When your parents were told, they were shocked and humiliated. They insisted you had never told them you were going to the church—who could imagine that a good Jewish boy, a boy who studies at *cheder* and helps his *tate* bake *challah*, could ever do something so wicked as to sneak behind his *mame* and *tate*'s backs to pray to idols? To listen to lies? Well, what do you have to say?

Yossele looked away from the rabbi, trying to find a sympathetic face—but there was none, just a tight circle of furious burning eyes and thick beards. His father was gripping the back of a chair so tightly that his fingers bled slightly. Shame suddenly welled up inside him, and tears burst from his eyes. He could not speak. He hated himself—he was an awful, terrible, wicked, disgraceful boy.

The rabbi's expression now softened. Child, do you repent? he asked. Do you promise to mend your ways?

Yossele nodded yes.

His *tate* walked over, smothered him in a warm hug, and kissed the top of his head. The men cheered and sang out blessings. Yossele cried and cried, but he felt happy that his days of hiding and shame had ended, and he could breathe easily knowing he was a good Jew again.

Yossele now was walked back and forth to *cheder* by his *mame* and never left alone during the Sabbath. But these precautions were unnecessary: Yossele was determined to avoid the church. He would not even look in the direction of its spire, and he spat on the ground and recited the *aleinu* prayer when he heard its bells ring. He focused his waking thoughts on the Talmud and Rashi's commentary, making every effort to incline his heart towards the Torah.

But Yossele could not control his dreams. Once asleep, he would drift far away from his warm stuffy home in the Rhineland, to an ancient rocky hill under a bright sun. A woman would approach him, tall and graceful, with thick black hair and sky blue eyes. She would tell him of her sorrow—her son had died, an awful death slowly bleeding from his wounds on the cross while the birds had pecked and gnawed at his flesh. And her son had been so full of love, love for everyone. He loves you too, Yossele, she would add. He loves you and despairs that you have run away from him. Go to him, Yossele, go to my son on the cross.

This same dream, with the same beautiful and sad mother, repeated every night for many weeks. Yossele begged the Holy One, Blessed be He, for different dreams, for righteous dreams filled with Torah, but his prayers were in vain. And with each passing night, he found himself more drawn to her and her lovely, mournful blue eyes. Yet he steadfastly forced himself to refuse her entreaties.

Yossele eventually sought out the rabbi, and asked what he should do about this dream. The rabbi answered Yossele in a firm tone: It is Lilith, queen of the demons, who haunts your dreams. The Wicked One, her husband Ashmedai, thought he had seduced you away from the Torah with the beguiling lies of the priest, but, having failed, he now sends his wife to use her beauty to tempt you at night, when you will be most vulnerable to your *yetzer ha-ra*, your evil inclination. I will write out a scroll for you with special combinations of holy names. Wear this scroll around your neck when you sleep, and the demon queen will be unable to assault your dreams anymore.

Yossele thanked the rabbi and swore he would never sleep again without wearing the scroll around his neck. But the scroll turned out to be impotent: she still came to him that night, just as on the nights before. However, this time, emboldened by the rabbi's words, he cursed her: You are Lilith, filthy demon, tempter into sin. I will not give in to your lures, and I banish you from my dream.

Yet the woman did not disappear. She sighed and hung her head. I am no demon, she said, I have been sent by God to help you. Can't you see that it is the men around you, in your waking life, who are the servants of the Devil? They want to keep you away from my beautiful son. You must resist them. Flee them.

And so his dreams now went each night: the woman denouncing his fellow Jews as lackeys for dark, infernal powers and begging him to leave his father for her son.

The rabbi asked if the scroll had driven Lilith away. Yossele lied and said yes. He was terrified of what the rabbi would think if he told the truth. So once again, Yossele's heart was heavy with shameful secrets.

He dreaded his dreams so much that he insisted, after *cheder*, upon studying late into the night at the *bet midrash*. He would sway over the Talmud in the dwindling light, refusing to go home even after the *shammes* had rebuked him sharply for wasting candles. Although he would devote all his efforts to staying awake, eventually sleep would overcome him. He would collapse on the rough wooden bench, and soon enough the same dream would return.

And then the day came when he saw the sad, beautiful woman from his dream in the waking world. It was a Tuesday morning, at *cheder*. A new student had come, a thin, small boy named Yoshke. His mother held his hand and presented him to the *melamed*, explaining sheepishly that he had yet to learn his Hebrew alphabet but he was a sweet little boy full of love. When Yossele, picked his head up from the tractate in front of him and looked over at the woman and her son, he was filled with terror: Yoshke's mother was the woman from his dreams.

Each day for the next week, this same woman dropped off her Yoshke at the *cheder*. Trembling and sweating every time he saw this apparition from his dreams, Yossele eventually decided to sneak out of *cheder* to follow her after she had left. She walked fast down a path leading away from the town and into the forest, before stopping to rest on a boulder by a spring. When Yossele reached her, she did not act surprised to see him but asked him to sit down next to her.

He obeyed her request. She took his hand and smiled. Her hand felt warm, even though the late autumn day was cold.

Why do you haunt me? he asked her.

She squeezed his hand and softly purred: Do not be scared. He loves you.

But this only made Yossele even more agitated, and he yelled back at her: But how do I know what you are?

She sighed gently and looked at him with compassionate eyes: If you feel God's light and warmth when I hold your hand, then you know what you need to know.

She squeezed his hand again, and he buried his face in her lap, trembling violently. She stroked his hair and then slowly pulled him up. Stand up and follow me, she said.

She led him through the forest, across meadows, and onto a road. They walked together until they reached a monastery at twilight. The woman knocked on the door and asked to see the Abbot.

The Abbot who appeared was a wizened old man in a coarse linen robe; he had a prominent forehead that gave him the appearance of being filled with wisdom and patience. When he saw the woman, he knelt down before her, and his lips kissed the ground by her feet.

She told the Abbot to rise. She entrusted Yossele to his care, ordering him to teach her son's ways to the boy, and to make him a monk. Yossele looked at the old Abbot and the elegant stone monastery building in the pink light of the setting sun. He felt a deep sense of peacefulness in every bone and muscle of his body. But when he turned back to look at the woman from his dream, she had vanished.

The next day he was baptized with the new name of Nicholas, and took up again the study of Christian texts and wisdom. He would at times feel an urge to return home, to be with his Jewish parents again, but at these moments he would see her again, the sad and beautiful mother, and she would stroke his cheek and hair, and assure him that he was on the path of truth and righteousness. She would speak to him of the love of his Heavenly Father, so much greater than the puny love of his earthly, flesh and blood father. Her sweet voice, and the bright light of her eyes, would soothe his homesickness.

In due course, Brother Nicholas took his monastic vows. He looked forward to a life of Christian piety and scholarship. The Abbot dispatched him to a different monastery of the same holy order, where they welcomed him warmly as a true brother.

But then his troubles began. The Bishop in that region had prevailed upon the local count to force his Jews to listen to a Christian sermon. It was agreed that Brother Nicholas, as a former Jew, should be the monk to preach to them; after all, he would know best how their erroneous thinking worked and how to show them the way to the truth, just as he had found the true path and abandoned the errors of Judaism.

Brother Nicholas protested he would be ill suited to this task. The Jews, he explained, had a particular loathing for converts to Christianity. They would be less willing to listen to him than to a priest who had been born a Christian. And he was a poor public speaker. He could better serve God in the cloister, helping with the gardens and copying manuscripts of holy books.

But his pleas fell on harsh, unkind ears. His fellow monks whispered cruelly to each other: perhaps Brother Nicholas feared his fellow Jews because he did not have a strong enough faith to resist the twisted logic of their lies. Or maybe he had never genuinely believed in Christianity, but he had become a monk for the cups of brandy and the roasted pork. Yes, the wagging tongues continued, he is a glutton—he only left the Jews to escape their prohibitions on the fine foods he wanted to eat.

The Abbot eventually sat down with Brother Nicholas to caution him that his stiff-necked refusal to preach to the Jews was leading to doubts about the sincerity of his faith and his conversion—although the Abbot was quick to add that he himself had full confidence that Nicholas was a sincere and believing Christian. But still, this sort of strife and backbiting was not fitting—brother should not mutter reproaches against brother. Nicholas was a young monk; he needed to learn to appreciate the importance of harmony within the cloister. It would reassure everyone if he would just preach the gospel to the Jews in the local synagogue. Whatever your fears, the Abbot said, have faith that God's light will fill your soul; it takes cunning to speak lies, but even the smallest children can speak words of truth.

Brother Nicholas relented. He now felt ashamed at himself for having hesitated to spread the true faith—how could he, he asked himself, be nervous about saying to anyone what was so obviously correct? What did he fear? And how would it look to the Jews if the brother who knew their doctrines best was afraid to confront them?

So he prepared his sermon. He racked his brain to recall the rabbis' proofs against Christianity, and their materialistic and literal readings of Biblical scripture, ignoring the Old Testament's higher spiritual and allegorical meanings that foreshadowed and proved the later coming of Jesus Christ. He wrote up detailed refutations of these rabbinical doctrines, consulting closely the works of other Jewish converts who had attacked the lies and errors of Judaism.

When at last he mounted the lectern in the synagogue, flanked by several armed guards whom the local count had thoughtfully sent as his escorts, Brother Nicholas felt certain his words would sweep away the Talmudic cobwebs tangling the souls of the town's Jews. He imagined their heads nodding in sudden realization of the truth when they heard his words, and that the sermon would end with a long, joyous procession to the baptismal font.

Yet as he launched into his well-rehearsed sermon, he looked out upon a sea of angry, sullen faces. He could see that their bodies were being held rigidly stiff and that their eyes burned with hate. When he was finished, the Jews quickly filed out in silence. No one looked at him, and no one sought the baptismal font.

Brother Nicholas felt humiliated, although he could not say why. He had done exactly what he had been asked to do: he had walked into the lion's den of the unbelievers and boldly declared the truth. But somehow he had become a fool for bearing witness to the faith of the Holy Church.

During the following weeks, his brothers at the abbey spoke little to him. He found himself sitting alone at mealtimes and kneeling alone at prayers. He tried to read but the letters swam about in his exhausted eyes. He only found comfort by lying very still in his bed and staring at a particular point in the ceiling where water damage had left the imprint of an egg shaped stain.

Yet even though he spent hours in his bed staring at the ceiling, sleep evaded him. In his fatigue, he would sneak away during the day to nap. He neglected his duties; he failed to be present for his prayers. Some of the other brothers upbraided him harshly for his indolence.

The Abbot finally suggested that he should perhaps stay, for a time, in another monastery of their holy order. And so Brother Nicholas left for a new abbey, relieved to be away from the men whom he felt had judged him with cruelty instead of Christian love.

At first, the change was salutary. The new cloister was halfway up a high mountain, near a deep blue lake, and the cool air gave him a new energy and determination. He labored happily most of the day in the scriptorium making copies of the Vulgate Latin Bible's Song of Songs.

Yet even in the mountain paradise, Brother Nicholas still could not escape the stain of his Jewish past. Several months after he had arrived at this new monastery, it happened that a small boy, with lovely golden hair, washed up dead on the shore of the lake. The corpse had deep puncture wounds in the chest and thighs, and had clearly lost much blood. The local lord ordered an inquest and appointed one his magistrates to supervise the investigation.

The matter dragged on. No culprits were identified; no justice was done. The magistrate opined that the murderers must have been passing robbers who had long departed from the mountainside. But the boy's parents would not accept this verdict. They denounced the magistrate as stupid, lazy, and corrupt. The other serfs eagerly egged them on, happy to see the haughty magistrate humbled.

And then matters took a turn for the worse. An itinerant preacher, clad in flimsy rags billowing about his skeletal frame, came to the village on the mountain. His eyes were wild with fury at the sinning all around him, and his tongue lashed out at the faithlessness of the world.

When this preacher heard of the beautiful boy's mysterious death, he insisted the local Jews were to blame. They have foul, devilish rites, he said; they murder Christian children to use their blood to bake their *matza* bread. The parents now demanded that the magistrate punish the Jews for murdering their child. The Jews, however, insisted upon their innocence.

The magistrate, the lord, and the Abbot conferred together. They needed an expert on Jewish ways, but one whom they could trust—a good Christian, whose faith would vouch for his honesty and integrity. And so Brother Nicholas was ordered by his Abbot to take over the murder investigation, as he alone among the Christians on that mountain intimately knew the customs, laws, and rituals of the Jews. He swore upon holy relics to go where the truth would lead him.

Brother Nicholas heard the evidence and acquitted the Jews. There were no witnesses or any other evidence linking the boy's death to any of the town's Jews. Moreover, as Brother Nicholas meticulously pointed out, Jewish law forbade the use of even animal blood in cooking, much less human blood. The allegation of ritual murder struck him as outrageous and absurd.

While the lord and the Abbot accepted his verdict, the serfs did not. The itinerant preacher denounced Brother Nicholas as a fraud, a latter day Judas who had again betrayed Christ to the bloodthirsty Jews. His loyalty, the preacher claimed, remained with the Jews who had raised him, and not with the Church to which he had sworn such apparently hollow and false oaths.

On the night after the verdict of acquittal, Brother Nicholas was woken from his sleep by sounds of screaming and yelling. He dressed quickly and followed the sounds to the abbey's courtyard, but there his brothers blocked his way. Brother Nicholas, they said to him, there is a large crowd, with torches and axes, and they are braying for your blood. They say you must be punished for your crimes along with the other Jews. Come, away from the gates, follow us.

They led him to an underground cellar, where they hid him in the darkness between barrels of brandy. There he spent a sleepless night, alone, listening to the taunts and shouts from the outer courtyard. He heard himself denounced as a liar, a Judas, a false Christian.

Eventually, the Abbot came to him with a candle; the light hurt Brother Nicholas' eyes. It is the hour of Prime, he said, and the crowd has dispersed. You are no longer safe here. In the courtyard there is a horse saddled and ready. Mount it and ride far away, now, before they return.

VIII. The Master of Repentance

BROTHER NICHOLAS RODE away with no clear idea of where he was going; he merely followed whatever roads seemed most familiar. He told himself he should find another abbey belonging to his holy order, but he could not bear the thought of speaking to another monk. How would he explain what had happened? His brothers would be deeply suspicious—they would be sure he had acted out of loyalty to the Jews; when God had tested his Christian faith, he had failed.

So Brother Nicholas avoided the abbeys he came across and slept instead in meadows and the occasional barn. He begged his meals from kindly peasants to whom he offered heartfelt blessings. It was a relief to see that the world still contained some good Christian souls. Or at least they were good and kind so long as they knew nothing of his Jewish birth.

After several weeks of aimless wandering, he came upon a town which looked quite familiar. Walking around the courtyards and the squares, and peering hard at the modest wooden synagogue, he realized that he had arrived back at his childhood home. He saw a group of boys running out of a low-lying, decrepit house at dusk, and recognized this was the end of their long day studying at the *cheder*.

In his monk's cowl with a heavy cross around his neck and the tonsure atop his clean shaven head, no one knew him. It felt strange to be back amongst the places of his childhood, yet not to be seen for who he was; the Jews who passed him in the street looked down and gave him a wide berth. But now he longed to return to his parents' house, to embrace and kiss his father, to devour a fresh, warm, soft *challah* loaf. Brother Nicholas yearned to be a Jew again.

Perhaps that was the lesson, he mused, of the murder trial. The Holy One, Blessed be He, had tested him, to see if he still cleaved to the truth and would resist the lies of the enemies of His chosen people. Like Job, his faith had been tested. He had rather faced persecution than falsely libel the Jews as murderers. He was one of the righteous of his generation. And he had proven himself not in the comfort of a *bet midrash* debating the finer points of the Torah, but alone in the lion's den of the most bitter enemies of Israel.

Of course, his thoughts rolled on, the horse had led him to this place. He had assumed he was wandering without purpose, but there is always a purpose—His purpose, the Holy One, Blessed be He, Who made the Heavens and the Earth, and Who chose this sacred people to carry out the commandments of his perfect and glorious Torah. He has brought me here to return to the bosom of my father, just as when Joseph was finally reunited with his father, Jacob.

It was dark now, and the moon was faint, but Brother Nicholas still knew these streets and alleys well and his feet led him to his parents' home. There was a light shining in a window of the small house, which heartened him. He knocked softly.

His father answered. Yes, Father, Priest, how may I help you? he said. His eyes were scared, and his manner was submissive.

May I come in? Brother Nicholas asked.

His father glanced nervously at his mother, who was standing nearby. After a long moment of silence, she nodded, and he was motioned inside the house.

He sat down in a chair in the front room. His parents stood in an opposite corner, trembling. He realized they must be terrified that a Christian monk had barged in upon them for no reason in the night.

Brother Nicholas smiled warmly at them. *Mame*, *tate*, he said, it is me, Yossele. I have come home. I wish to repent, to return to the true path.

His parents remained silent for several minutes. He could not figure out what they were thinking. After a while, Brother Nicholas stood up and approached his mother to embrace her, but she flinched and averted her eyes.

He turned then to his father, who gestured to him to go into the kitchen and sit down at a wooden table. There was no light there, and he had to rely on the flickers from the candle in the adjacent room. At that moment Brother Nicholas was flooded with love for his father. He thought he could see specks of flour still clinging to his father's beard from the day's work in the bakery, and he could smell the warm, earthy sweat from his father's hairy chest. He had an urge to bury his head in that chest. But when he looked into his father's eyes, there was no warmth or kindness.

Why have you returned, Yossele? Do you think your mother wants to see you like this, in your Christian robes?

Brother Nicholas inhaled deeply to steady himself. *Tate*, he began, I know I have sinned and I wish to repent. I have embraced lies that I thought were the truth. I saw such powerful visions of Mary, mother of Jesus, she spoke to me, and I thought it was the truth. But she lied. She must have been a demon.

I lived with them for years, I learned their ways, and I bowed down to their idols. I even preached their lying words to righteous Jews, may it never happen again. But recently the Holy One, Blessed be He, opened my eyes again and exposed their wickedness to me. A terrible libel had been hurled against the Jews near my abbey. A wicked Christian preacher, a true Haman, had accused the Jews of murdering a Christian boy to drain his blood for baking *matza*. I was ordered to investigate and pass judgment, as I was the only Christian in the area with any knowledge of Jewish ways.

I saw immediately that the charges were abominable lies. I demonstrated the flimsiness of the evidence, and I explained how the accusations are contradicted by our holy Torah. While the lord of that region accepted my judgment and acquitted the Jews, the Christian peasants seethed with rage. They surrounded the monastery's walls, and demanded my blood be spilled in vengeance. The other monks kept me safe for the night, but then sent me away in secret in the morning—they had no desire to defend my verdict, even though it was just.

I rode away with no destination in mind. I begged for bread and slept in fields. And as I wandered, my soul felt lost. I did not wish to return to the Christians. There were many churches and monasteries along the way where I could have lodged, but I avoided them all.

And then the Holy One, Blessed be He, in His infinite and abounding wisdom and kindness, led me here, to the town where I was born, where I had lived as a Jew should live. When I saw these same streets, when I heard the chanting of Talmud study from the *bet midrash*, I knew that I had been brought back here by *HaShem* to return to the Torah. I will cast off these disgusting robes, do my penitence, and return to the people of Israel.

Despite the passion of his words, Brother Nicholas noticed that his father's grimace had not softened. He waited now for his father to respond, hoping that he would walk over, call him Yossele again, and hug and kiss him.

But there were no tender embraces. His father eventually replied: Do you recall, now that you remember being a Jew again, hearing *parsha Balak* chanted in the synagogue? Maybe the Hebrew words have slipped your mind—maybe they made a bashful exit to make room in your head for all those new Latin words that you had to learn. So I will remind you. Balak, King of Moab, commanded the prophet Balaam to curse Israel. But the Holy One, Blessed be He, would not permit Balaam to curse His chosen people and instead forced blessings to issue forth from his mouth. It was the same with you: you serve Moab, but your mouth is forced to issue praises of Israel. It was not your wisdom that acquitted the Jews of the false charges of murder—you have no wisdom, you are a fool, you chase after phantom women in your dreams and abandon your flesh and blood mother, who has shed rivers of tears over your wickedness.

After we learned that you had been baptized, we begged the Holy One for guidance. Like Job, I railed against His might and His will. What had I ever done to merit such an evil only son? You were to be my *kaddish*, to make me a grandfather, but you brought me nothing but shame and suffering. What sin had I committed that was so terrible that I should be cursed with being the father of someone like you?

My grief tore me apart, but my anguish was nothing compared to your mother's broken heart. She had carried you inside her body, nurtured and suckled you from her own flesh, and this is what you had become? Was my milk so sour, she asked me again and again? Was my milk poisoned?

Our rabbi here told us to accept the will of the Holy One, Blessed be He, and to have strength enough to believe that you would return someday and repent of your sins. But I said to him: How can my Yossele ever return after sins such as these? It is not as if he stole a sack of potatoes. He has prostrated himself before idols and served the persecutors of Israel.

One day, the Holy One answered my pitiful prayers, and showed me the truth of matters. A scholar came to our town. He was learned not only in the outer Torah of the law, the *halachah*, but also in the Torah that is concealed—the mystical truths hidden beneath the surface meaning. This man wandered from town to town fasting and battling demons and working miracles.

When this scholar came to our town, he insisted upon seeing me immediately. To what do I owe such a great honor?

I asked. This saint, this *tzaddik*, he said to me: I came to this place to comfort you. I had heard of your sufferings, and I had invoked the holiest of secret divine names to compel the Throne of Glory to send me a messenger to answer my questions. When the angel appeared before me, I asked why an upstanding Jew such as yourself had been cursed with such a loathsome abomination for a son.

And here is what the angel told me: There were once two souls in the Treasury of Souls in the World to Come. One was righteous and pure; he was supposed to be your child—a true Jewish soul, a beautiful Jewish soul, whose mournful chanting would one day make the Heavenly Court weep in despair for Israel's many sufferings in exile. The other soul was wicked and cruel; this soul, the angel recalled, had a foul smell and a slimy black texture. But when it was time for these two souls to descend from the World to Come into their earthly mothers' wombs, Lilith tricked the angels and switched them. Your wife's womb did not receive the holy Jewish soul, but the wicked soul.

You labored tirelessly to bend your son to the path of Torah, but you cannot make a cockroach soar through the clouds like an eagle. When your son grew to be a man, Lilith called to him to return to her and her demon filth, and so he was baptized. But the angel told me you should not despair, because in the World to Come you will be reunited with the righteous soul of your true son, who will love and honor you the way a true Jewish son loves and honors his mother and his father.

So you see, Yossele, or Brother whatever you call yourself before the idolaters, you are not my son. You cannot return to my home because you should never have been here at all. Somewhere out there, trapped in a Christian body, lives my real son and his Jewish soul. And he will come to me, eventually, in his proper time. But you, you I cast off as unclean, as filthy *treyf.* You are wicked to the core.

You say now you want to return to Israel, but for how long? Until Lilith whistles in your ear again and flashes her pretty eyes? You have not seen the truth in the Torah. You were shamed before your fellow Christians because, as He did with Balaam, the Holy One worked the miracle of blocking curses from passing the threshold of your lips. But you will hunger again for their praises, and for their honors and riches. Your tongue will water at the thought of chewing their succulent pork. I will not mistake you for my son again. Be off with you and never return.

His father stood up and pointed towards the front door of the house, his chest heaving violently up and down and his eyes quaking with hatred.

Brother Nicholas felt as if his father were speaking of someone else—it could not be possible that his father truly meant such cruel words for his only son. But as his father remained steadfast in his wrath, Brother Nicholas's heart grew heavy and he felt a harsh, sharp chill run through his limbs.

He pleaded his case one last time: But *tate*, it is me, your son, Yossele. I did terrible things, committed horrible sins, that is true, I admit it. I have wronged you, I have failed to honor you as my father. I am guilty. I must beg your forgiveness. But I am a Jew, just as you are. A sinner, but still a Jew—Jonah sinned when he fled from the Holy One's command, but he was still a holy prophet of Israel. Please, please do not drive me away—I need the Torah again—I need it to sustain me. How can a soul be wicked, in all times and places, no matter what its deeds? How can the Gates of Repentance be forever closed against its face?

But his father's only response was to walk over, grab the hood of his son's robe, drag him across the floor, and toss him back over the threshold into the dark night. Brother Nicholas did not resist. He wept as he walked through the town's empty alleyways—not a monk's philosophical melancholy tears at the world's fallen state, but a little boy's geyser of self-pitying tears that flooded his eyes and blotted out his vision.

The next morning Brother Nicholas found his way to an abbey and rejoined his holy order. When he learned of the need for a confessor in a remote castle, in an impoverished, forgotten corner of the Holy Roman Empire, he immediately volunteered for the posting.

IX. Idol Worship

BROTHER NICHOLAS OFTEN paced the castle walls through the sleepless nights. And when he did sleep, Cartaphilus's angry rebukes reverberated through his dreams. Sometimes the ancient, undying Jew strapped to his cross in the castle tower morphed into his father or his town's rabbi. But their words were always the same: he had been placed under a *cherem*, a ban, and cast out from the people of Israel. He had no share in the World to Come.

Nor was the Church any comfort: they, too, had cast him out for telling the truth, had hounded and persecuted him. He struggled to understand how such calamities had come to pass. He had only wanted to pursue truth and to learn wisdom. He had opened his heart to the divine presence wherever he felt it. And still, he had been spurned as a traitor by both Church and Synagogue.

He considered the castle ramparts. The drop was steep. He would be assured a swift death. The pain would be brief. But this would be no help. As a suicide, he would be damned whether Jew or Christian. His soul would be wrenched violently from his crumpled, broken corpse by demons with fiery whips who would scourge and torment him on the way to his eternal punishment.

One night, Lady Catherine approached him on the ramparts. She was alone. The wind rustled her long, loose black hair. She took his hand in hers.

Brother Nicholas, she said, I see you brooding on these walls every night, ever since you visited with Cartaphilus. Did his words trouble you? You should not let him anger you. His curse and his wandering have made him coarse and spiteful. He delights in making others share his bitterness.

Brother Nicholas remained silent. But he found the softness of the skin of her hand to be a comfort.

Did he mock you for taking baptism? she continued. Denounce you as a traitor to your fellow Jews? I can see it in your eyes. Your brothers in the Church suspect you are still secretly a Jew, but the Jews despise you as a traitor.

That is why you were led here, whether you knew it or not. My master can give you the grace and love that you long for. Come with us, pray to him, and take his Eucharist in the forest. Your suffering will dissipate like a morning fog, and you will feel nothing but joy.

She squeezed his hand and rested her chin on his shoulder. A biting wind tossed clumps of her thick perfumed hair upon his cheek and lips. The strong fragrance made him light-headed, but happy—her presence soothed his bitterness.

In the moonlight, he could see her smile—a queen's smile of satisfaction that her subjects adored her.

Eventually, he broke the silence: Lady Catherine, I cannot bow to idols or drink blood. But I will serve you faithfully.

Come with me then, she said. She led him by the hand down from the walls and through the courtyard to her brightly lit suite of apartments. That evening she directed him to write several letters, to the Bishop and his former Abbot and various and sundry other churchmen. In these letters he described the inhabitants of the castle and its lady as faithful, devout Christians. He wrote of his success in persuading the noble household to hear Mass daily and to make full and sincere confession of their sins. When he was finished, a servant took the cache of letters to be sent out by messenger the next morning.

Lady Catherine now reclined on a couch and took Brother Nicholas's head into her lap. She stroked his cheek. Looking up at her face, he thought she looked like a statue of the Holy Virgin Mother come to life to comfort him in his misery.

He did not know how long they stayed this way, in peaceful quiet, but at some point he fell asleep and then later woke in his own bed. The sun was bright; he had slept late and no doubt missed the morning Mass. He washed and dressed quickly, ate a light breakfast, and went to attend to his duties in the chapel.

That night he joined Lady Catherine and her attendants for dinner. Even though he had lately preferred to eat simple meals of barley bread and hard cheese in his rooms, now he felt an urge to see her, even if he had to endure being mocked again. To be near her, to smell her strong perfumes, was his heart's whole desire.

But there was no mockery this evening. She gestured to him to sit next to her. She asked him trivial questions about the weather or the chapel, and cast approving smiles in his direction. She took his hand for a time and pressed her leg against his under the table. He felt a rush of excitement, a giddy dizziness, but it was good—there was no shame or guilt.

Afterwards, Lady Catherine invited him again to their Mass in the forest. But again he said no. Much as he longed to be near her and to please her, the thought of drinking blood made his body retch and recoil. He remembered his *mame*, when he was little, cooking pieces of meat on a Friday afternoon for *Shabbat* dinner. She would kindle the flames repeatedly to make the meat cook faster, racing against the setting of the sun when cooking would no longer be permitted. But *mame*, he would say, the meat is done. No, Yossele—if there is even one drop of blood left in it, it is forbidden to us to eat.

He could not drink blood.

Lady Catherine did not press him further, but instructed him to go to her apartments and wait for her return. He mutely obeyed.

When she returned from her black Mass, she dismissed her servants; Brother Nicholas alone would wait upon her that evening. She ordered him to undress her and run her bath. Once more he quietly obeyed. He stood bashfully in attendance as she stretched out naked in her tub, luxuriating in the fragrant rose water. Yet he had no desire to lay with her. Instead he felt a deep awe of her, as if she were a being from a higher realm whose blessing he sought.

When she was finished with her bath, he helped her to dry, dress again, and brush her hair. Because her locks were so long and thick, brushing them was a long, arduous process. There were a surprising number of tight little knots lurking here and there; he realized, with a slight shock, how little he actually knew of women's hidden labors to keep themselves so pleasing to the eye. His wrists were quickly exhausted from the repetitive labor, but he forced himself to continue until he had brushed out each knot.

Now she directed him to make her bed, which he promptly did. She lay down under the covers and dismissed him with a warm smile.

And so began Brother Nicholas's new routine in the castle. There was no longer a Mass in the morning, as he would still be asleep, but he would attend to his clerical duties from noon until sunset. At night, he would not join Lady Catherine's dark rites in the woods, but he would wait upon her afterwards as if he were her manservant instead of her priest. He felt joy when she displayed signs of her approval and felt devastated when she flashed the slightest feeling of unhappiness or irritation. With each passing day, he noticed something new and wonderful about her—the shape of her lips, the curves of her hips, the easy grace of her walk, the way her mantle snuggly enfolded her voluptuous chest. Yet their relations were entirely chaste, and Brother Nicholas never tried to lay with her.

Sitting at Lady Catherine's feet abjectly adoring and admiring her brought him a deep, fulfilling sense of peace. He felt that her eyes were filled with a tender, maternal love for him, and forgiveness. Not that he had wronged her and needed her forgiveness for some particular misdeed; no, she somehow forgave him all his sins, for his whole life through, forgave him everything he had done and offered him absolution without guilt or condemnation.

The past and the future both slipped away from his mind. He thought that this was what the Garden of Eden must have felt like to Adam: an eternal present, with no notion of time passing—just a floating, rippling serene delight in the beauty around him.

X. The Passion of the Jewish Monk

ONE AFTERNOON, LADY Catherine seemed troubled. She would not look at Brother Nicholas, and she breathed so heavily that the sound was like a hiss. He tried to speak of bland pleasantries, about how she had slept and the humidity of the late afternoon sun, but she ignored him.

The atmosphere at dinner was tense. There were no smiles, no laughs, and no music. The lovely youths and maidens stared down at their plates. After eating in silence for several minutes, Lady Catherine abruptly stood up, walked across the room, and grabbed the chin of one of her handmaidens. She lifted the young woman's face up so that their eyes met. The young woman trembled, but when she tried to look away, Lady Catherine struck her on the cheek.

Finally, Lady Catherine spoke: How could you have let this happen? What fool here loosened his chains?

The maiden, still shaking, answered her in a cracking, faltering voice: I cannot say how it happened. He was chained to the cross, like every night, and the door was bolted. But then he was gone.

And now Brother Nicholas understood: Cartaphilus, the cursed, embittered eternally Wandering Jew, had escaped. No, escaped was the wrong word: he had apparently simply left, as if he had grown tired of a banquet that had dragged on too long. All the time he had been held in this castle—certainly months, perhaps longer—Lady Catherine had been able to use Cartaphilus's endlessly replenishing, honey sweet blood for her rites. This had been her solution to the horrible demands of her lord: no more killing, no more lingering guilt; she could harvest and imbibe human blood without sin. Indeed, having been cursed by Jesus Christ Himself on the *Via Dolorosa*, Cartaphilus's sufferings were divinely sanctioned. Lady Catherine, in her way, had been serving the Church.

But with the Wandering Jew's disappearance, Brother Nicholas's thoughts continued, Lady Catherine's soul would be stained again: she would be forced once more to murder innocents to appease her master. There had once been a time when he would have thought this her just recompense—her pact with whatever vile demon she served had led her into sin, and eventual perdition, with her only hope being to abandon her wicked ways and to repent, even if that meant bodily suffering and deformity in this world.

But these sentiments now struck him as petty and base. He wanted her to stay eternally beautiful, even if that meant she must continue to drink blood, and regardless of whether she merited good or evil. The more wondrous a creature she was, the less he suffered. Her joy had filled him with joy, and the warmth of her smile had washed away all the grievances of his past.

On a sudden impulse, he jumped up from his seat and began shouting: Drink me! Drink me!

Lady Catherine loosened her grip on the maiden, and turned to face him.

He continued: Yes, drink me. Even if he is gone, you do not need to sin, you do not need to murder. You can take me, willingly, I give myself to you. I will take the sin of my death upon myself alone, so that you can be blameless. I will be your sin offering.

She answered him calmly: Brother Nicholas, that is very noble of you, but you do not need to do this. We will find others, just as we have before. You should join us in eternal life, as I have told you so many times. Take our master's Eucharist and become one of us.

But he would not desist. He demanded, ever more loudly, to be sacrificed. He wanted to die so she could live. She told him the wine had overheated his brain, and suggested he retire to rest in his bed. When he persisted in standing next to the table, gesticulating feverishly and begging to die, she slammed her fist down upon a plate and ordered him to leave her presence.

Yet the more that Brother Nicholas reflected upon his desire to sacrifice himself, the stronger that yearning grew within him. To offer himself up on the altar would be the greatest testament to his faith. Abraham was a mighty saint for obeying a command to sacrifice his son, but how much greater the test, and how much greater the show of faith, to sacrifice yourself—like the Christian martyrs who had defied the demands of the pagan Romans to bow to statues and worship false gods. Or like the holy Jewish saints in the Rhineland in the year 1096, who willingly slaughtered themselves for *kiddush hashem*, sanctification of the holy name, rather than be baptized by the Crusader Knights.

Church and Synagogue had both failed him, but she had taken him in and loved him. She had bathed him in her light. He imagined Lady Catherine drinking his blood, his body and soul dissolving into her. Through whatever strange magic she harnessed from her lord and master, she would transmute his blood into pure, extended life—no, into more than just breathing and waking life: into beauty, into smooth skin and thick hair and soft lips. He could join with her, become a part of her beautiful form.

When Lady Catherine finally ran out of Cartaphilus's blood a few days later, Brother Nicholas fell at her feet before her bed and again begged, with hot tears streaming down his cheeks, to give his life to her—for her to drink him up.

She looked down at him, so far beneath her on the ground, but he no longer saw irritation or impatience in her eyes. Her expression now seemed to mix sorrow, pity, and compassion. She sighed, and smiled slightly. Then she crouched down and wiped his tears away with her palm.

Do you truly love me so very much? she asked.

His only response was to shiver and quake. She wiped his cheeks some more, and let her hair fall sloppily upon his neck and shoulder.

If this is your heart's desire, then so be it, she said.

Lady Catherine left the room. He remained on the floor, frozen, waiting for her return. When she came back, she was accompanied by the two lovely young maidens who had drained Cartaphilus's blood. Lady Catherine reached down and gently took Brother Nicholas by the hand. She helped him stand up and led him outside into the warm night air.

The two maidens walked ahead as she led him into another tower and down the steps, to the room where Cartaphilus had been kept. Seeing that room, he felt a sudden blast of doubt. Maybe he did not want to die—to kill oneself was a sin—the Holy One, Blessed be He, had said in the Torah: I give you a choice between life and death, choose life. And what would happen after death? His soul would burn in torment, punished for his many and terrible sins, suicide chief among them.

But why live? His love for the Torah had been unrequited; his love for the Church too had been unrequited. But this marvelous woman had shown him true compassion. He must return her love and prove his faith in her. To willingly go to damnation for her everlasting beauty: that would be the sanctification of her name.

The maidens strapped him to the same cross where they had bound Cartaphilus, first the left arm, then the right arm, and finally his feet. He did not resist. This was how Isaac was, he thought, when Abraham tied him to the altar, meek, yielding, and joyful, because he knew the importance of his sacrifice. He would be the scapegoat for Israel's sins forevermore and bear witness for them before the Throne of Glory in the World to Come. So too shall I, he thought, be the scapegoat for her sins and bear witness for her in the next world.

One of the maidens fetched the wide bowl they used in their black Mass in the forest. She stood next to him, ready to catch his blood.

The other maiden came forward with the lance with which she had pierced Cartaphilus's side. She handed it to Lady Catherine. Without a word, Her Ladyship drove the spear-point deep into his ribcage.

The pain was terrible at first. He screamed—he could not help it. Lady Catherine held the lance steady, seemingly indifferent to his cries. After a while, as his blood poured out—he heard the steady pitter-patter as it fell into the bowl—his head became light and dizzy. The pain was so great that it exhausted his ability to feel anything at all, and he started to go numb.

He used all his remaining strength to look at her. He thought he saw her looking back at him with such love and gratitude in her eyes. And his last gesture was to smile. That was how he died upon the cross: with a wide, serene smile on his face.

Other Books by Barak Bassman

Elegy of the Minotaur

Repentance: A Tale of Demons in Old Jewish Poland

King Solomon and Ashmedai: A Wisdom Tale

The Twilight of the Magical Siren: A Tale of Late Antiquity

The Leper Princess and The Court Jew

The Last Confession of Joseph della Reina

The Gifts of the Fairy Melusine

Necromancy of the Demon Maiden:
A Gothic Tale of Podolia

The Death of the Wizard Merlin